DARE TO BE THREE

THE DARE MÉNAGE SERIES
BOOK THREE

JEANNE ST. JAMES

Jeanne
ST. JAMES

Editor: Leanore Elliot

Cover Art: April Martinez

www.jeannestjames.com

Sign up for my newsletter for insider information, author news, and new releases:
www.jeannestjames.com/newslettersignup

THE DARE MENAGE SERIES

The Dare Ménage Series:
(All can be read as standalones)

Double Dare
Daring Proposal
Dare to Be Three
A Daring Desire
Dare to Surrender
A Daring Journey

CHAPTER 1

He was dark. So dark, the rich, deep tone of his skin reminded her of a ripe plum. She couldn't ever remember seeing someone quite so black. Because of this, her gaze kept drawing back to him. It was rude to stare, she knew, but she didn't seem to have any control over it. She couldn't keep her eyes off of him.

His head looked smooth and beautifully shaped. He had the type of structure which made bald look good.

Never a fan of facial hair, Paige Reed rarely liked it on a man. But this man's goatee was neatly trimmed and fit his face perfectly. A thick gold hoop earring hung from his left ear. He wore a well-tailored suit. He probably had no choice but to get his suits either made for him or, at the very least, tailored to fit. His shoulders were broad, his thighs thick.

She thought her brother-in-law was built like a beast, but this man outsized him. He was enough to intimidate anyone crossing his path.

But not Paige.

He fascinated her.

"You find him attractive, don't you," her husband's whisper came, close to her ear.

Not posed as a question, but she answered anyway, "Yes."

"I'm not sure why you married me, then. I'm as pale as a person can get," he teased.

Paige brushed her fingers through Connor's dirty blond hair, ruffling it a bit. "No, you're not. You worship the sun. And it was that sexy Aussie accent of yours that caught my attention."

"It made you wet."

Paige half-shrugged and gave him a smile. "Still does."

Connor brushed away a strand of hair from her cheek. "Hmm. Good to know. But you like him."

"He's *interesting*."

"He's dark," Connor stated.

"Yes."

"His skin tone is extraordinary. I like it too."

"Should I be jealous?" she asked.

"Should I?" Connor's vibrant blue eyes twinkled.

Paige laughed, shaking her head. "We've talked about this. Jealousy is not allowed."

"I wonder what he'd say if he knew what we were talking about."

"Or thinking," she added.

"He'd probably run like hell."

"I don't know. I'd hope not." Paige regarded the man across the room talking to her brother. "I've never seen him before. I wonder how well the guys know him?"

"Could be Quinn's friend. Or a former co-worker of hers," Connor suggested.

"Coming to Ty's fortieth birthday party? I doubt it."

"Maybe he's related to Ty."

"*Maybe* we need to stop speculating and ask," Paige suggested.

"You want him." Again, not a question. Just more of an, *are you sure?*

"Do you?" she asked.

"I like what I see. But I need to find out what's up here." He tapped his temple.

Suddenly, Tyson White slipped between the two of them and squatted. Even though the man had retired from the NFL years ago, he was still in extremely good shape, and his shoulders were wide enough to brush against them both.

Not that Paige was going to complain. She and Connor always flirted with Logan's boyfriend, now husband. But it was always in good fun. Ty loved it and neither Logan or Quinn, their wife and mother of their child, minded.

Ty cocked his eyebrow at Paige. "Why are you staring at Grae like a piece of meat?"

"Was it that noticeable?" she asked, surprised.

"Uh, yeah. Hard to miss."

Paige shrugged. "He's hot." *Grae.* What an interesting first name. She wondered what it was short for. Maybe it was a nickname.

Ty looked behind him for a second at the subject in question, then turned back to Paige. "Yes, he is."

"Who is he?" she asked. "Current or former player?"

"Retired. Sort of. Left the NFL after a debilitating medical issue."

"Like what?"

"Like, I'm not telling you his secrets. You'll have to find out for yourself. And anyway, why are you guys so interested?" Ty asked, suspicion thick in his question.

Hmm. The man was a mystery she might have to solve.

Connor spoke up, "Well, you know, there's a certain man I've been trying to get into my bed for a couple years now, but for some reason, he keeps resisting."

Ty lifted his left hand and pointed to his ring finger. "I'm married if you've forgotten."

Connor chuckled. "I haven't."

"And I have a kid." His face lit up. "And another on the way."

"Oh, shit. Congratulations! You sure Quinn wants everyone to know?" Paige asked him.

"You aren't everyone. You're family. But keep it on the D.L. since it's early yet." Her brother-in-law pushed himself to his feet and stepped back from the table. "C'mon. I'll introduce you to Graedon. I won't warn him about the depraved things you two are probably planning for him."

"Oh *please*," Paige retorted as she stood and took Ty's arm on one side, her husband's on the other.

Ty escorted them over to Paige's brother, Logan, who had been deep in conversation with this mystery man.

"Hey, hot stuff," Ty greeted his husband. "Should I be jealous that you've been talking to this handsome hunk of a man for an hour now?"

Logan offered his hand, and Ty took it. Logan drew the darker man into his side, his arm slipping around his waist.

Darker, Paige thought, but not nearly as dark as this...*Graedon*. She liked the name on her tongue.

And that wasn't the only thing she'd like on her tongue.

Wow. She shook her head. She normally wasn't this depraved. Something about this man just drew her in like a fly to honey. Paige held out her hand. "Hi. I'm Logan's sister, Paige."

Graedon gave her a slight smile and, with a quick flick of his eyes, looked her up and down—didn't *that* make goosebumps flood her body—before clasping her offered hand within his.

His grip felt warm and firm, and his hand dwarfed hers. Paige marveled at the contrast of their skin. Their clasped hands reminded her of a yin and yang symbol: opposites, but complementary.

Connor cleared his throat.

Paige released the man's hand, heat climbing into her face, though it seemed Graedon was in no rush to break the contact either.

Logan waved a hand towards Connor. "Grae, this is my brother-in-law, Connor Morgan. The poor sap stuck with Shorty."

Paige glared at her older brother. He knew she hated that nickname.

"Shorty." The name rolled smoothly off Graedon's tongue, and he seemed reluctant to pull his attention away from her to shake Connor's hand. The men's handshake was quick and firm. "Graedon Ward," he introduced himself to Connor.

"Interesting first name," Connor told him.

"Interesting accent," Graedon remarked.

"Connor is Australian," Ty explained.

"And Shorty's husband," Connor said, jerking a thumb towards Paige.

Paige whacked him in the arm. "You know I hate that nickname!"

"Well, I can't tell him my other pet names for you." Connor smiled at Graedon and wiggled his eyebrows.

"He's got a thing for brothers," Ty warned Graedon.

Graedon looked over at Connor in surprise. "Oh?"

"He's not the only one," Ty added, tilting his head toward Paige.

"I'm sorry. I didn't mean to stare so rudely," Paige said, grimacing at Ty's comment.

"Okay then! On that note, we need to go mingle, old man," Logan said as he drew the birthday boy away.

"You're older than me," Ty griped.

"But I look younger," Logan said, as they moved away.

Paige's gaze bounced back to Graedon. "So..."

"You don't mind your wife staring at other men?" It was a serious question but touched with a sense of amusement.

"Well..." Connor pursed his lips for a second. "It depends."

"On what?" Graedon asked, once again clearly surprised.

"On who she's staring at."

Graedon shook his head, obviously confused. "You're not worried she might be interested in the man she's staring at?"

"Oh, I definitely know she's interested in who she's staring at."

Paige waved her hand between the two of them. "Hello! I'm standing right here. Jeez."

"I'm truly sorry, Paige," Graedon said, bowing his head to her. "That was rude of us."

She blinked. Rude? Not unlike her staring.

Now, since she stood next to him, she realized how large a man he truly was. Though she *was* small, or nicely put, petite, hence the "Shorty" nickname. She had to look from her five-foot-two inches up to Connor's six-foot-one. But this Graedon, he had to be an inch or two taller than her husband. While Connor wasn't skinny, the other man definitely outweighed him by— Paige guessed—at least fifty pounds. His hands were large, his fingers long. Good for gripping a football, of course. She wondered how old he was and how long ago he left the game. "How do you know Ty?"

"We played football together in college."

"Ah. And you went on to be pro?"

"Yes, I was lucky enough to be drafted."

"You retired?"

Graedon hesitated for a few seconds, then answered, "Yes, a while ago."

All right, she didn't want to keep bombarding him with questions. She definitely wanted to get to know him better, but she didn't want it to seem like an inquisition.

Oh, but she had so many questions on the tip of her tongue.

What do you do for a living now? How old are you? Do you live around here? Would you like to have sex with my husband and me?

The last one might be a little much. She certainly didn't want to scare him away. And here she thought she would be bored at Ty's fortieth birthday party, but then she spotted his man. She realized she was staring again and her face became heated. "I need to get a drink. Anyone else?"

"I'll get it, honey," Connor said, placing a hand on her shoulder. "What do you want?"

"Something with alcohol. Surprise me." Connor knew her tastes well, so she wasn't worried he'd come back with a drink she didn't like. *Wait.* Had she ever met a drink she didn't like? *Oh, yeah. Gin and tonic. Blech.*

"Anything for you, Graedon?"

"A gin and tonic, please. Thank you." He gave Connor a wide smile.

Paige swore it just lit up the whole room. Of course, he would want a drink she hated. But she wouldn't judge him for it. Much, anyway.

"I'll be back shortly," her husband said, kissing her cheek then heading toward the makeshift bar in the corner of the large room.

Her eyes never left Graedon while her husband kissed her—while his, in turn, never left hers. Until her nipples beaded under the thin fabric of her dress—then his gaze dropped but quickly returned to her face.

"I don't know how you can drink that awful shit."

"It's an acquired taste." He studied her face.

Paige tried not to squirm as he ran his gaze from the top of her head to her chin, then just high enough to land on her lips. She unconsciously licked them and then tugged on her bottom lip with her teeth. "I don't think any drink that you need to learn to appreciate is worth drinking. So many other choices."

He stared at her mouth while she talked. She fought the urge to dig into her clutch purse to reapply her lip gloss.

"Choices are wonderful, but sometimes you want one specific thing. So, you work for it until you achieve it."

"We're still talking about drinks, right?" she asked.

He finally raised his eyes to meet hers as a wince of surprise and then clarity flickered in his gaze. Like he'd shaken himself mentally, getting out of some sort of fog.

She hoped it meant that he felt attracted to her.

Suddenly, he leaned toward her, and she froze. He reached out and whisked away something on her face with his thumb.

She stared at him curiously.

He held his thumb up. "Eyelash. Make a wish."

Paige knew exactly what she would wish for. She pursed her lips and blew lightly, the eyelash spinning towards the floor.

"I hope your wish comes true," he murmured, not breaking their locked gaze.

"Me too." Little did he know *he* was her wish.

The seconds ticked by and neither even blinked.

His eyes were like very deep wells of dark brown. Dangerous if you fell in. His thick eyelashes were surely the envy of some women. His lips were dark and thick, reddish at the center like he'd been sucking on a cherry. Those luscious lips parted...

Paige waited for the words to escape, to flow over her. She just knew he was about to say something intriguing.

"Sorry, there was a line at the bar." Connor approached, handing her a tall glass filled with pinkish-red liquid, a maraschino cherry, and a tiny plastic straw. He handed Graedon a short glass filled with ice, a lime wedge, a stirrer, and the clear toxic mix that made Paige scrunch up her nose.

Graedon nodded at Connor, thanking him.

He was such a gentleman, but one she bet knew how to be not-so-gentle at the right times. She covered her sigh by sipping on her drink. She had no idea what the concoction was, but it tasted fruity, and it went down smooth.

Connor upended a beer bottle and took a swig. Some local microbrewery. No piss water—what Paige called regular beer —for him.

"So, what do you do for a living, Connor?" Graedon asked after squeezing his lime wedge and stirring his drink.

Connor slid his arm around Paige's waist and gave her a small squeeze.

Graedon's eyes followed the gesture and didn't raise until Connor answered.

"I'm a structural engineer."

Graedon contemplated the answer. "Structural. Like bridges?"

Connor shrugged slightly. "Yes, bridges. But I mainly concentrate on sports complexes. Like stadiums, arenas, and what not. Anything sports related."

Graedon raised his eyebrows. "Football stadiums?"

Connor nodded. "Yes, some."

"Sounds like a very interesting career."

"It is. But I have to travel a lot."

"Is that how you met your stunning wife?"

Stunning. *Huh.* Paige never considered herself stunning. This had always been a description for leggy blondes who strutted down runways. Cute, maybe. She was short, with long brown hair. Then add some freckles, which didn't make sense for her complexion. Her whole family had been confused about this. Mailman's daughter, Logan had always teased her, which had always upset their single mother.

But it did make her wonder. Especially, since Logan was a foot taller than her and didn't have a single freckle.

Connor gave her a look before answering him, "Yes. We actually did meet at a football stadium. She was with her brother when he was there to re-sod the field."

Paige remembered that day. Logan's business was just getting off the ground and, since she'd been helping him with the business's books, he had asked her to go along because he didn't have any employees at the time. It had been long days laying sod, and they were both filthy and exhausted come nightfall. She was happy she no longer helped with the physical part of the business.

Then, she reminded herself, if she hadn't gone, she never would have met the crazy, sexy Aussie, who currently had her pinned to his side. The rest was history. Connor picked up his life and moved to the States, gladly making her hometown his, and they got married a few years ago.

Now, with Quinn doing the books and Ty as Logan's partner, the business was extremely successful, and Paige did whatever the guys needed her to do, either on the sod farm, in the office, or out on a job. A sort of Girl Friday/project manager with a great salary and benefits. If they needed coffee, she got coffee. If they needed her on site at a sodding job supervising employees, she was there. The job was never boring. The guys and Quinn relied on her. Sometimes to simply babysit their son Preston.

"Best day of my life," Connor stated, giving her another squeeze.

"Yes, you're certainly a lucky man," Graedon said slowly, the words rolling off his tongue like molasses.

"You could be too."

Paige elbowed her husband. *Too soon.*

Graedon tilted his head and studied Connor. "What do you mean?"

"I just meant one day you'll meet the girl of your dreams." Connor tripped over his words as he added, "That's if you're not already married. I shouldn't assume."

"I prefer women over girls. And, no, I'm not married."

Paige's gaze flicked to his left hand. The only ring this man wore was the one in his ear.

"Yes, a woman," Connor murmured. "One that knows what she wants, when she wants it, and how to get it." He shifted his left arm up to her shoulders.

Once again, Graedon followed his movement until he pinned his gaze to Paige's lips once more. "And you, Paige?"

And me what? Oh. "I help out with Logan and Ty's business."

"I'm sure that keeps you busy. Their business is extremely successful."

"It is. Who expected growing grass could be so lucrative?"

He cracked a slight smile. "I'll have to come out and tour the farm one of these days."

Paige tamped down the urge to rub her palms together in anticipation. *'Will you walk into my parlor?' said the Spider to the Fly.* "Yes, please do. Just let me know, and I can personally escort you."

Graedon tipped his head graciously.

"She's crazy behind the wheel of the UTV. So, I'm warning you now…"

Graedon looked confused. "UTV?"

"Utility Task Vehicle. Like an ATV for farm use," Paige explained. "However, don't listen to him. I have a safe driving record." *'The way into my parlor is up a winding stair.'* "You'll be perfectly fine in my hands." *'And I've a many curious things to show when you are there.'*

"I'm sure I will be," Graedon murmured.

'Oh no, no,' said the little Fly, 'To ask me is in vain, for who goes up your winding stair-can ne'er come down again.' "Why don't I give you my number, and you can text me when you want to come out."

His smile appeared and then disappeared as quickly as it came. A blink and it would've been missed. "Only if your husband doesn't mind."

"Connor doesn't mind, do you, honey?" she asked her husband, without even so much as peek his way.

"No, not at all."

Graedon dug out his cell from an inner pocket of his suit jacket. A few seconds later, he was ready. Paige didn't hesitate to spill her digits.

"Morgan?"

She shook her head. "Reed. I didn't change my name."

Once again, he cocked a brow. Paige thought this might be a signature expression for him.

He slipped his cell back inside his jacket and pulled out a business card. "So you know it's me calling."

Paige tried to pluck it from his fingers, but he resisted just enough so her hand had to make contact with his. The brush of their fingers made her suck in a breath and warmth radiate from her core.

Damn. If this was her reaction to just a light touch, she couldn't imagine how she would respond to something more substantial. But she didn't want to imagine; she wanted to *know*. She let her hand drop, the card ignored in her grasp.

Connor placed his left hand at the small of her back and extended his right hand out to Graedon. "Excuse us, we need to go visit with Quinn. I don't want her to think we're ignoring her tonight."

The larger man shook Connor's hand, then turned to Paige. He dipped his head. "It was nice meeting you tonight. I look forward to the tour."

"It was nice—" *staring at* "—meeting you also. Hopefully, it'll be soon."

Then with that, Connor steered Paige out of earshot. "What do you think?" Connor asked her, barely-contained excitement in his voice. "He's intelligent, well-spoken, hot as fuck."

"Oh, he's a big fat yes. But I wasn't getting any vibes from him other then he's a het."

"Yeah, he was hard to read except when it came to you. He was definitely drawn to you. I think I should be jealous."

Paige bumped her shoulder into him as they walked. "Stop. If you need to make the rules, then make them. If I meet up with him and you don't ever want me to have sex with him without you, then I'll agree to that. I don't ever want you to feel left out, honey."

"We'll discuss it. We'd have to find out if he has any proclivities toward men. If not, that shoots the plan all to hell."

"Plan? Now we have a plan?"

"You had a plan the first second you laid eyes on him across the room, whether you knew it or not."

Paige pursed her lips in thought. "Yes, you're right. As soon as I saw him, I knew I wanted him."

"See?"

"But I want to try to get to know him better if he comes out to the farm. And I have this." She lifted the business card so she could read it. "You could always ask him out for a business lunch or coffee."

"I would need a good excuse other than, 'my wife and I want you to join us in bed.'"

Paige snorted. "You never know, maybe he likes direct."

"Yeah, like he wants to take you directly to bed. He's definitely fascinated by you as well."

"Well, that's a good start."

Connor pushed his way through French doors which opened to a dark patio. Outside, the breeze felt cool, and Paige shivered.

Connor removed his suit jacket and wrapped her in it, pulling her into his arms. "So, what does his card say?"

She held the crumpled card up. "Too dark to read it."

Connor lifted a hold-on-a-second finger and dug his cell phone out. With a push of a button, the card was illuminated.

Paige tried to smooth it out a bit and peered closer. "Graedon C. Ward, College Scouting Director, Boston Bulldogs."

CHAPTER 2

Paige wasn't surprised when she got a text from Graedon two days later. She hadn't stopped thinking about him since Ty's birthday party. She and Connor had discussed what their plan would be if he didn't contact her within the next couple weeks, or, more importantly, what she would do if he did.

When her phone vibrated, and she saw the message, she had forwarded the text immediately to her husband with shaky fingers. Her heart had beaten furiously until Connor called her, hardly a minute later.

To say they were excited would be an understatement.

Now, as she waited out in front of one of the farm's outbuildings, the official offices of *LGR Sod, Inc.,* she tried to tamp down her anxiety. Which was a bit hard to do since her stomach was doing flips like she'd been jumping on a trampoline.

She didn't even want to wait for him in her office, so she'd grabbed a UTV and parked it out front in anticipation. And she paced next to it. She glanced at her watch at least a dozen times. He didn't seem to be the kind of person to be late. Ever.

She glanced up when she heard tires crunching on the gravel driveway. She quickly moved to the UTV and leaned against it, pretending to be as cool as a cucumber. He was five minutes early. Yep, just like she thought, he was probably never, ever late to an appointment.

A black BMW X6 with dark tinted windows approached her, kicking up dust behind it. He'd most likely have it washed by the end of the day since she couldn't imagine him driving a car with a film of dust on it. Especially that beautiful vehicle. It fit what little she knew about him perfectly. Paige sighed. She not only wanted him, but she also wanted his vehicle now too. She giggled at her own ridiculous thought, but it helped her relax a little bit.

One thing she appreciated almost as much as men were cars. Powerful, well-designed, sexy cars. Powerful, well-designed, sexy men. Both irresistible.

Graedon pulled up to her, stopping parallel to the UTV. He rolled down the driver's side window.

Her breath caught unexpectedly when he came into view.

"Hey there."

"Hey." *Act normal, Paige. Don't run up to the vehicle, rip open the door, and haul his ass to the ground, straddling him, to strip him naked. Deep breaths.*

"Do you want me to park anywhere in particular?"

Yeah, I need you to park your body on top of mine. She shook her head. "No, just…wherever."

With a sly smile, he tipped his head and rolled the window back up before parking at the side of the building.

Paige moved so she could watch him unfold himself from his BMW. The man was simply *big*. Tall, solid, and…*oh fuck*…the muscle on him… Paige reached out blindly for the four-wheeler to keep herself from collapsing to her knees.

He wore a navy long-sleeved Henley that fit him like a second skin. There was no guessing on how built this man was. The fabric clung to every curve of his arms and chest. He must spend hours at the gym. Though neat and clean, his jeans were worn; the denim looked as soft as room-temperature butter. Touchable. His thighs appeared thick, and she was surprised the seams of his jeans hadn't split yet. He may no longer be playing in the NFL, but he sure looked like he still trained for it. Squats and sprints. That's how you got heavily muscled thighs like his.

She noticed his sensible boots as he came closer while her breathing seemed to shallow.

When he stood near enough, he put a finger under her chin and closed her mouth.

Paige swallowed and stared up at him towering over her.

"How are you?" he asked with an amused smile.

"F-f-f-ine." Paige cursed herself. She was acting like a lust-sick idiot.

He cocked a brow. "I won't harm you."

What? Paige shook her head, confused. Had he thought her reaction was fear and not her actually melting in her panties?

"In case you're worried since we're alone together," he explained.

Worried? He should be worried about *her* if he only knew the thoughts rolling around in her head. She finally shook herself out of her stupor and laughed, the tinkling sound rising around them. "Thank you for the reassurance, but I wasn't worried about that."

"Some women are afraid of black men," he said matter-of-factly, studying her face carefully, his eyes narrowed.

She frowned. "Why?" This might just be the stupidest thing she ever heard. Okay, maybe not *the* stupidest, but it was up there.

"You tell me. You're a white woman."

Was he serious? Was this some sort of test? "I have no fear of men just because of their skin color. That's ridiculous."

"Maybe it's something instilled from way back in the day. Passed from generation to generation through some families." Though definitely a serious subject, he was attempting to make it lighter than it was.

That would be fine with her since this was not how she

planned to start their time together today. "All the way back to cotton-picking days," she joked, though half-heartedly.

"Maybe."

"Well, I don't care what color a man is if he's scary. I've been cornered plenty of times when I was younger, afraid I was going to get sexually assaulted or worse. And you know what? They were all white men. No, not men. Boys. Thinking they could do whatever they wanted to me. Like I was a piece of meat. Something not human, something to be used for their convenience, their pleasure."

"I'm sorry."

"You have no reason to be sorry." Paige looked at him closely. "Unless you've done the same type of thing. It's inexcusable. I wish parents would raise their sons up to respect women."

"There are a lot of men who respect women."

"A lot isn't *all*. There's a difference."

"Understood," he said, with a curt nod of his head.

Then with that, they stood there, carefully observing each other. Well, that conversation just dampened her flaming desire. Now it was at a low simmer. *Shit.*

"I'm sorry, Paige. I appreciate your offer to show me sod. It's a very interesting business."

Paige threw her head back and laughed. He had a dry sense of humor, and she liked it.

He pinned his lips together, but he couldn't hide the smile. His eyes gave it away.

"Well, let's hit it. I'll drive."

"Someone warned me about your driving," he said, climbing into the passenger side of the utility vehicle.

"I haven't killed anyone yet," she replied with pride in her voice.

"Sounds reassuring." He searched around his seat. "Does this vehicle have seat belts?"

"Nope. Just hang on." She tapped the black metal tubing that held the roof up on the machine to show him where to grip. "Here we go. You're getting the first class tour of *LGR Sod, Inc. Where the grass is always greener.*"

Graedon chuckled.

The sound rippled along Paige's spine, and her nipples tightened. "No, seriously, that's the slogan."

She decided to drive like a sane person instead of her normal speed as if she were in a qualifying NASCAR race. She didn't want to scare him and give him a reason to cut the visit short. As they proceeded away from the building, she kept on the beaten path out through the sod fields.

She snuck a glance at him. He had such a strong profile, his gold earring flashing in the late morning light, his freshly-shaved head perfectly smooth, his goatee trimmed short and neat. She wanted to test how prickly those short hairs were. "So, Mr. Graedon C. Ward, College Scouting director of the Boston Bulldogs, tell me about yourself."

His gaze remained intense as he studied her.

Turnabout is fair play, she guessed.

"I'd rather talk about you." His voice dripped like warm, dark molasses. Smooth, deep flavored, but not sweet. It had a bite to it.

"I'm boring." She didn't want to talk about herself. She wanted to hear him speak until that voice coated her until she was sticky.

"I highly doubt it. What do you want to know?"

Anything. Everything. "What are you willing to tell me?"

"How about whatever question you ask me, you have to answer the same question," he posed.

Paige thought that could become interesting. But she was willing to play. "Okay. Let's start simple. How old are you?" She putted along the edges of the sod fields, heading to the farthest field on the farm. One far, far, *far* from the house and the offices. She decided to take the long way around.

"Thirty-eight."

Her gaze shot to him then back to the dirt road. He sure didn't look thirty-eight.

"What? Do I look older than that?" he asked, a touch of humor in his voice.

"Are you fishing for compliments?" Paige arched her brow.

His laughter enveloped her, warming her as she drove the windowless vehicle. Dressed similarly to him, she wore a long sleeve T-shirt and jeans, but the temperature was a little chilly for an early spring day.

"And you and Connor?"

"I turned thirty a few months ago, and Connor just turned thirty-four. What made you quit football?"

He hesitated. "I didn't quit. I was forced to retire. And I'm not going to answer that one since you can't answer a similar question."

Paige tilted her head in deference. At least, she obtained one more piece of his puzzle. He retired because he was forced to. And he didn't want to talk about it. Yet. Maybe she would have to Google his football career. "Okay, fair enough. How many siblings do you have?"

"Three."

She shot him a look. "Brothers? Sisters? Where are you in the line?"

"I'm the eldest. I have two sisters and one brother. How about you? Any siblings other than Logan?"

Paige snorted. "Logan is plenty, thank you very much. And I'm *younger*."

Graedon laughed. "I already knew that answer, so I get a freebie."

"Fine," she said, shrugging.

"Why are you interested in me?"

Paige gripped the steering wheel a bit tighter. Within thirty seconds, they finally reached the farthest edge of the property, and she stopped the UTV along the line of maple trees that butted up against the field. She shut the engine off and took a couple of soothing breaths before turning in her seat to face him.

When she met his gaze, she was swallowed up by the serious look in his eyes. She caught her bottom lip in her teeth.

Graedon reached out and pulled on her lip, brushing his thumb across it before moving away.

That small touch shot lightning through her.

"You haven't answered the question," he prodded.

"I don't know. I'm not sure why. I saw you and something just pulled me. I can't explain it."

He nodded slightly as if he understood. Maybe he'd had the same sort of instant attraction to them as they'd had with him. "Your husband seemed to like watching our interaction the other night."

Paige shrugged nonchalantly. "Yes, he did."

"Is he a voyeur?"

Paige laughed softly. "No, he's an active participant."

"But he's heterosexual?"

Some male partners liked to watch the females in the relationship have sex with other men. Connor said he wouldn't mind watching, but that wasn't his goal. He loved sex, the intimacy, the physical connection as much as Paige.

"Umm." Paige sucked in a deep breath. There was no reason to beat around the bush. She had him out in the middle of a field, at least a mile from his car. He couldn't escape anywhere. It was kind of the perfect situation to lay their desires out in the open, per se. "You didn't notice how he looked at you also?"

"I noticed. I wasn't sure what to think," he said softly. At least, he hadn't run through the fields screaming. So far.

Cautiously, she asked, "Did it bother you?"

"Should it have?"

He was hard to read. She couldn't tell if the idea was not to his taste, or if he felt curious. "You're answering a question with a question."

His words were extremely firm when he said, "And you're not being straight with me."

She felt slightly admonished by his tone. Clearly, this was a man who didn't like games. "Sorry. It's sticky."

Graedon brushed away a lock of hair that had blown across her cheek. "It doesn't have to be. Just spill it."

Once again, her body reacted to his simple gesture. "Connor is bi-curious. He's had a thing for Ty since they met. Ty would have been his first if Logan wouldn't have killed Connor and buried him out in one of these fields. Logan is very possessive of Ty. Quinn too, of course."

"That's to be expected."

Paige shrugged. "Sometimes it's a bit much."

"Men want to protect what's theirs."

Not all men. And men aren't the only ones. There were many possessive women out there. Dangerously so. "As long it doesn't become smothering."

He didn't seem to agree or disagree with her, which made her wonder how possessive he could be. "So, back to your husband."

Right. "Even though Connor is curious and attracted to men, he's never had the opportunity to hook up with the right one."

Graedon's eyes widened, and he leaned back in his seat. "Are you suggesting that I'm the right man?"

"I don't know. Are you?"

He stared at her and said nothing as he searched her face. Paige sat very still, trying not to reveal her desperate hope that he *was* the right one.

"What gave you the inkling that I had even a remote interest in men sexually? Or even threesomes?"

Paige's stomach dropped.

Then before she could answer, he continued, "And you are clearly not talking about a ménage à trois with two women."

"No."

"Do you really think I'm here today to tour a bunch of grass fields?" He cocked his eyebrow.

Nobody in their right mind wanted to look at boring sod. "No."

"So why would you think I'm gay since the tour was just an excuse to see you again?" He reached over and slid his fingers along her jawline until he buried them into her hair.

His palm felt warm against the side of her face. "Not gay," she murmured.

"Definitely not gay. I have a great interest in the woman before me." He leaned towards her while pulling her closer. He held his lips above hers, barely a breath between them. "So, is it a package deal? I can only have you if I have Connor too?"

She wanted to say no because she wanted nothing more than him at that moment. He mesmerized her, put her in some sort of corporeal trance when he got this close. His eyes made unwavering contact, his voice, low and deep, his breath a warm breeze over her lips. She willed him to close the gap. Though, the true answer to his question was yes. And no matter how much she desired this man at this second, she could never forget about Connor. Never would. She blew out the breath she held. "You want one; you get both. No compromise."

"I see." He released her and sat back in his seat, putting some distance between them. "Have you done this before with someone else?"

"No."

"Was this an impulsive decision?"

"No. We've been talking about this for a while now. We see what Ty, Logan, and Quinn have together. And what Ren, Eve, and Cole now have. Do you know them?"

"Yes, I know Renny and Cole well. I've only met Eve once. They have quite the chemistry."

"Then you know what we're looking for."

His brows pinned together. "Not quite. Are you talking a

serious relationship? Or are you looking for someone for Connor to experiment with?"

Paige didn't know what their final destination would be. She and Connor had only wanted to test the waters first. See if it would even work for them. Three people in one relationship took more work than the typical couple. And a lot of couples weren't even successful, so the failure rate for a threesome was extremely high. Especially, if there was any sense of unevenness or jealousy involved. It could even end up that Connor found men weren't for him and he might shut the whole idea down. Yes, he was attracted to certain men, but when it came down to the nitty gritty...

However, Paige was walking into this situation knowing what would be involved. She'd watched the other threesomes' relationships develop and grow. It wasn't for everyone, that was for sure. Her only fear was if the third person would come between her and Connor. It would be the last thing she wanted. "Is that what you're looking for?" she asked him.

"You're the one opening the door. I'm just the person on the other side waiting to be invited in."

She thought about the meaning of what he just said. He seemed very intelligent, and she couldn't imagine him mincing words. "Well, it's not like I wanted to come out and ask your sexual preferences. That would be rude."

"But you're asking me now. Just in a more convoluted way. So, you don't think it's rude at this point? Do you think we suddenly know each other well enough?"

Heat crawled up Paige's neck into her cheeks. She placed her palms on her face, trying to cool her skin.

"Sorry. I'm being blunt." He pulled her hands away from her flushed face. "I'm attracted to you, Paige, and I know you're attracted to me, which was apparent the other night. There is nothing I'd rather do more right now than pull you out of this vehicle and take you completely in that soft grass. In truth, that was my intention when I came. But you know nothing about me.

We've known each other for…" He glanced at his watch. "For maybe an hour total."

"We could get to know each other," she suggested.

"Which is why I am here."

"But you still haven't indicated if you're interested in Connor, even in the slightest bit." Maybe they'd been grasping at straws, maybe Graedon was one hundred percent heterosexual. But something niggling at the back of her mind made her think otherwise. Perhaps it was his lack of reaction at her mention of taking them as a couple, and not just her. Most heterosexual men would have reacted differently. Wouldn't they?

"I am friends with everyone you mentioned earlier, all in multi-partner relationships. It doesn't bother me. I see how when it's great, it's spectacular. But I've also known people in polyamory relationships where it went horribly wrong. Are you willing to risk your marriage? Because that's what you'd be doing."

"Honestly, I'm hoping to enhance our relationship, not damage it. I'm not the only one who is interested in this. Connor needs no convincing. If he weren't the one who suggested looking for a third, then I never would have even considered it."

"But you are a willing participant."

She nodded. "Very much so."

"The two of you caught my attention the other night, whether you know it or not. I saw you from the other side of the room, long before I talked to Logan. In fact, I queried Logan who you were."

Paige felt surprised. Logan had given no indication of this. Though maybe it was because Logan had become less protective of her, once Connor had entered the picture. It was like her older brother had handed over the reins to her husband. It was now Connor's job to keep her safe. "Just me? Or me and Connor?"

"Both. You two left no doubt you were a couple. And I would never approach a woman who wasn't single without some indication it was welcomed by both parties. I was pleased when you two showed interest."

"So wait..." Paige scrubbed her face with her palms. Was she hearing him clearly? "You *are* interested?" She dropped her hands into her lap. Was this really happening? *Holy shit.*

Graedon picked her hand up and examined it, tracing his fingers over hers, sliding a thumb across her palm. "Yes, I am."

Paige's brain spun like a hamster on an exercise wheel. Deep down she really never thought he'd agree. It seemed like a long shot with horrible odds. But he said yes.

He said yes.

She had no idea how to approach the situation from this point on. Though, his next three words made Paige's stomach drop.

"Under one condition..."

Paige realized she had been holding her breath. She released it in a rush.

"I'm allowed to have sex with you without Connor being there, and the same would go for him. If I want you on a Sunday at midnight, I get you at midnight on Sunday. Understood?"

Paige's heart raced. Would Connor agree to that? "And the two of you? Would you want to have sex without me?" She couldn't imagine Connor having sex with another man without her. But she couldn't be sure.

"That option could be explored later. It may never even get that far. If Connor is bi-curious like you say he is, then this sexual *experimentation* of his may quickly change his mind."

Damn, she hoped not.

Maybe she was just being selfish, but the thought of her being spoiled sexually by two men was a hell of a fantasy. The image of this man and Connor being those two men made her pussy clench. "Do you want to explore right now?" She had a hard time keeping her voice from shaking with anticipation.

"I would like nothing better, but I think we should wait for your husband."

His use of "your husband" should have disturbed her, but it didn't. It excited her more. She whispered, "I already got permission from him. I would never be with another man without him okaying it. I love him too much."

Graedon raised his eyebrows. "You two have a weird relationship."

"That may be so, but it works for us."

"I see. I would love to have the two of you over for dinner. We could get to know each other more and then proceed from there."

"We would love that."

CHAPTER 3

Connor rang the doorbell as they stood outside of Graedon's front door. "He didn't say if he was bi, or gay, or whatever?"

"Connor, you've asked me this a hundred times. No," she whispered loudly.

Paige tried to have patience, but Connor acted so nervously and fidgety... like a kid who ate a pound of candy and then was told to go to sleep.

Connor was mouthing, "This house is really nice," when the door opened and the man who had invaded her wet dreams the past few nights stood before her, the glow from the foyer backlighting him, so he appeared as a dark silhouette.

"Come in." His deep voice resonated through the early evening air.

The sound made her shiver. With a wide smile, she shoved Connor through the door and followed him into the house.

"Good to see you again," Graedon said as he shook Connor's hand, then took their coats.

Paige kicked her shoes off.

Lowering his gaze, he regarded her discarded heels on his

spotless ivory-colored marble floor. "You don't need to remove your shoes."

She could have sworn he'd said, "Make yourself at home."

No? Oh, well.

"Oh, yes I do. If I could go through life barefoot and braless, I would. Nasty torture instruments made by someone without a vagina."

Graedon cocked a brow and glanced over at Connor, who just shrugged and said, "*Women.*" As if that explained everything.

Graedon nodded and hung their coats in the foyer closet. Paige thought she heard him chuckle softly when his back was turned.

"You've got a beautiful house." She surveyed the wide stairs flanked by wrought iron handrails leading up to the second floor and the crystal chandelier hanging from the vaulted foyer ceiling. She moved to the right and peered into a room. A large stone fireplace with a huge flat-screen TV over it was the centerpiece of the wide room. Football players scurried across the screen until a whistle blew.

Graedon swept by her, grabbing the remote. "I apologize. I was catching up on some game film. Attempting to find a diamond among chunks of coal."

Connor held up his hand. "Wait. Don't turn it off yet. What game was that?"

"State versus Clemson."

Connor nodded his head, and settled on the couch, his eyes never leaving the screen. "Yeah, I remember that game."

"Are you a college ball fan?" Graedon asked, studying Connor's face.

Connor paid the other man's scrutiny no mind. So much for him being nervous. "I watch some. I prefer NFL games."

"Who's your favorite team?"

The question was weighted, but Connor answered without thought or hesitation, "The Bulldogs, of course."

"Of course," Graedon murmured. "Can I offer you two a drink?"

"Just one?" Paige joked.

Graedon shot her a wide smile. "You may have as many as you'd like. As long as you're not driving."

Good point, but a little bossy. Paige chewed her bottom lip.

"Don't." The word was sharp.

With a start, Paige released her lip. *What. The. Fuck.*

Connor looked up confused. "Don't what?"

Graedon waved his hand. "Nothing. Sorry. What would you like?"

"A beer, if you have it." He went back to watching the taped game.

"And a gin and tonic for you, Paige?"

His suggestion lessened her tension. "Oh, yes. I'd *love* one."

A chuckle rumbled from deep within his chest. "Why don't you accompany me and I'll give you something you'll enjoy. We'll be right back, Connor."

Paige glanced at her husband who looked way more relaxed than he had all day. All it took was a little football. *Men.*

With a quick shake of her head, she wrapped her hand around Graedon's offered arm. She marveled how small her hand actually looked on his arm. He wore a thin emerald green V-neck sweater that, once again, emphasized every muscle above his waist. She gave his bicep a squeeze as he led her out of the living room into a game room off of the kitchen.

A beautiful, carved wood pool table sat front and center, a bar lined the back wall, and, in one corner, was a poker table. Another huge TV hung from the wall. A pair of French doors led out to what appeared to be a deck. It looked too dark outside for Paige to be sure.

Without warning, Graedon backed her against the wall, placing both palms flat on either side of her head. She smothered a surprised gasp as he leaned in, his chest pressing against hers.

She could feel the rise and fall of his breathing. Being so close, she inhaled nothing but his scent. Sandalwood, maybe. And testosterone. Her nostrils flared as her body recognized the latter and it warmed her core.

Without her heels, she felt even smaller next to him. He could overpower her, make her his, and she would be unable to do anything about it. The thought hardened her nipples to painful peaks and her breathing shallowed. She wondered what it would be like to just let him have all of the control.

"Are you ready for this?" he asked, his voice deep, growly.

"Dinner?" she whispered breathlessly. "Sure."

"No. This." He cupped her cheek in his hand and closed the slight gap, his lips taking hers. They were warm, broad, and silky soft, but oh-so-demanding. He kissed with the same confidence he exuded. He tilted his head for better access while pressing his large, solid body even tighter against her. His tongue teased along her lips, coaxing them open. And when she obliged, he took her mouth completely, wreaking havoc on her senses. She groaned into his mouth, and he tangled his tongue with hers, demanding her total attention.

He released her lips abruptly, pulling back just enough to say, "I can't wait to slide inside of you, give you everything you want, desire, and beg for." His eyes were dark, his pupils wide.

Her chest rose and fell quickly as if she were starved for oxygen. She swallowed hard as she trembled, on edge.

She couldn't wait either.

A clearing of a throat brought her back to reality, but Graedon didn't push away. He continued to stare into her soul, making her squirm.

"Kissing my wife..." Connor said from the other side of the room. His hair appeared mussed as if he'd ran a hand through it once or twice. His face looked flushed.

Paige couldn't tell if he was pissed or excited with what he witnessed.

Without moving away, not even turning his head, Graedon said, "That's what you brought her here for, wasn't it?"

Connor didn't answer until he moved farther into the room, closer to the two of them. "You're right, it was. I've never seen her kiss another man."

"Did you enjoy it?"

Connor ran a hand over the front of his jeans where it bulged. "I did."

Graedon pushed away from Paige, turning his back to her as he moved behind the wet bar. He opened a small fridge and pulled out a beer. He twisted off the top and offered it to Connor. "Do you want a glass?"

Connor shook his head and moved up to the bar. "No. Thanks." He took a long pull from the bottle, then placed it on the marble bar top.

Paige hadn't moved a muscle. She remained pinned against the wall, though no one or nothing held her there. She wasn't sure how Connor would react catching them kissing and felt pleasantly surprised there were no signs of jealousy. A good start for sure.

"My turn," Connor stated as he rushed across the room and smothered her lips with his.

His mouth was wet, cool, and flavorful from the cold beer. Her husband had never been this rough with his kiss before. Where had this man been hiding? Their sex life was awesome, and nothing had ever been lacking, but tonight, after seeing Graedon kiss her, a fire burned within him. A strangled moan escaped her as he dug his fingers into her hair, pulling her head back. He caught her bottom lip between his teeth and gently bit down. She melted against the wall and reached between them, finding him hard and ready.

He straightened and brushed a knuckle over her cheek bone. "I want to watch him fuck you." His voice sounded low and rough, his eyes hooded.

Paige stared at him in surprise. "I need you to be one hundred percent sure."

With a quick nod, he backed away from her.

"I want to hear you actually say it, Connor."

"I'm sure, babe. Just watching you kiss him did it for me." He grabbed her hand and pressed it against his zipper. "You can feel how hard I am."

Paige snuck a peek at Graedon. He leaned against the bar, a drink paused at his lips.

She quickly stepped up to the other man, grabbed the glass out of his hands, and downed the contents in one swallow. She slammed the glass onto the bar top. "Damn, that shit is nasty." She wiped the back of her hand over her mouth.

"I can make you something you'd like. Simply say the word," Graedon said, watching her with amusement.

She popped her hands on her hips and looked up at him. "Did that do it for you, too?"

"It did."

"Good." She moved behind the bar and looked at what he had in stock. "I need a Long Island iced tea or something strong. No foo-foo drink."

Graedon came behind the bar to stand next to her, pulling bottles off the shelf. "I can make you one. Then we can move into the kitchen and have dinner."

She grabbed the bottom of his tight sweater and yanked it up enough to see his well-defined abs. Then ran a finger along the indentations of his muscles. "Fuck dinner. We have more important things to do."

"Like you?"

"Yes, like me. Connor wants to watch."

As Graedon poured various types of alcohol into an ice-filled pint glass, his eyes flicked to Connor. He stirred the contents and took a sip before handing it over to Paige. "Perfect," he stated.

Paige wasn't sure if he referred to the drink or the idea of

Connor wanting to watch. She swallowed a mouthful, the sweet and sour drink going down smoothly.

"I'm not going to complain that I get her to myself the first time," Graedon said to him.

"Don't get used to it," Connor replied, returning to the bar to pick up his beer.

Graedon arched an eyebrow and gave Paige a look. "You did tell him my conditions, right?

"Yes, we discussed them," she answered while regarding her husband. He had agreed with them at the time. Did he change his mind?

Connor took a deep breath, then said, "I heard your conditions. I'm out of town a lot, so I get where you two would want to get together when I'm away."

"I also travel often due to my position, so I want to make it fair, and make sure there are no hard feelings."

Connor nodded his head. "Maybe that's what we should agree on. If I'm out of town, it's okay. If I'm in town, I have to be included. Same for you."

Graedon placed a hand along Paige's lower back. "I'll agree with that if Paige does."

Paige shrugged. "Hey, I can't bitch about that. I'm the one benefitting here." She took a long drink from her glass.

"Whoa, you need to slow down there, babe," Connor said, a worried look in his eyes.

"Why don't we go relax? I'm not sure if you heard, but Paige suggested skipping dinner for now and—"

"Get busy," Paige interrupted Graedon.

"Yes, apparently the phrase is *get busy*."

"Seriously, you were a football player in *locker rooms*, how can you not use slang or even curse?" she quipped. He seemed a bit uptight when it came to the English language. Little did he know that she was a professional potty-mouth. He would figure it out soon enough.

"Paige curses enough for both of us; she'll sear your ears," Connor warned him.

True, but... "If you're going to be offended by my creative use of the English language, then this may not work out."

"I won't be offended," Graedon said. "Just because I choose to speak a certain way, doesn't mean you can't be yourself around me. It's important we all feel comfortable with each other."

Why did she get the niggling feeling that he'd done this before? What would the odds be that they picked someone who had more experience than her or Connor when it came to multiple partners? Hell, they had zero experience with multiple partners. Only fantasies. Maybe having someone with expertise would be an advantage. Now that she considered it, if he had been in a relationship or situation like this before, what happened to it? What went wrong? *Shit.* Paige chewed her bottom lip.

"Every time you do that, Connor or I will have to distract you. You shouldn't bite your beautiful lips."

Beautiful lips? Huh. "Distract me, how?" She got a feeling she knew what he meant, but she wanted him to show her anyway.

"Like this." He reached for her hips and pulled her close, kissing her hard and quick.

Connor came up from behind, sandwiching her between them. With his hands on her waist, they both turned her around, and Connor whispered, staring at her mouth, "And this." He kissed her fiercely, taking his time, unlike Graedon. He lifted his lips long enough to say, "You taste so good," before taking her mouth again.

Being kissed by her husband while another man pressed against her from behind was so...*erotic*. And she realized this was only the beginning.

Graedon brushed her hair away from her neck to blow his warm breath against her heated skin. His mouth followed, his tongue sliding along her spine, stopping only when he reached the neckline of her sweater.

He felt hard against her ass, and it was difficult to miss how large he was. From what she could tell, even with denim separating the two of them, he was much larger than Connor. And Connor was no joke either.

Graedon's hands slid from her hips down to the globes of her ass, squeezing them together as he thrust against her. He found the back of her neck again, sinking his teeth softly into her flesh.

Paige pushed her ass against him while leaning into Connor, grabbing her husband's biceps to steady herself. She groaned into his mouth as Connor played with the peaks of her nipples through the soft, knitted fabric. Hard and sensitive, she wanted someone's mouth on them.

But the three of them were fully dressed, standing behind a bar in a game room. This was not where she wanted to be taken by another man in front of her husband for the first time.

She flattened her palms on Connor's chest and pushed him slightly. "Where?"

Graedon smoothed his hands up her ribcage until he cupped her breasts from behind. He murmured against her skin, "Follow me."

Though slightly disappointed when Graedon stepped back from her, she knew it wouldn't be long before he would be touching her again. Her breathing became rapid and shallow as Graedon took her hand, leading her from the room, back to the foyer, and up the stairs. Connor gripped her other hand as she pulled him along.

Not that he needed urging. Excitement and anticipation filled his eyes, and he couldn't keep his free hand off his hard cock hidden behind his denim.

Paige felt tempted to watch him because whenever Connor touched himself it turned her on, but at the pace Graedon traveled up the stairs, she was forced to keep eyes forward to make sure she didn't trip and accidently tumble all of them down the steps.

When they got to the landing of the second floor, Paige's heart began to beat furiously. They were only steps away from this happening. She quickly peeked at Connor and squeezed his hand.

He squeezed back, giving her a nervous smile.

Connor had always been her rock. He needed to keep his shit together so she could. But Paige felt like a virgin about to get her cherry popped.

At the end of the hall, Graedon opened one side of double doors, sweeping his arm toward the interior of the bedroom, indicating they should enter. "Welcome."

Something in that welcome held such promise it made Paige even more nervous. Graedon seemed to be rock steady, not a nerve in sight. He'd definitely done this before. He acted way too comfortable with what was about to happen.

The bedroom looked oversized, like the man standing in the center of the neat-as-a-pin room as he observed her and Connor's reaction. The king-sized bed was made up perfectly, not a wrinkle or a loose corner in sight.

Paige bet the room had a luxurious en-suite bathroom and a walk-in closet big enough for her to live in.

The rich colors consisted of tans, creams, and browns, with a little burgundy to highlight. Someone put a lot of thought into decorating this master bedroom. Paige loved it. And it fit its owner. Tasteful, refined, but subdued. "Beautiful," she whispered.

"Thank you. My interior decorator understood my requirements and hit it out of the park."

"How long have you lived here?"

"Paige, really," he admonished her. "Do you want to spend time asking me unimportant questions or would you rather me undress you?"

Well, when he put it that way…

Graedon indicated a curved upholstered chair in the corner. "You may sit there to watch."

Connor looked where he suggested and then back to Graedon. "And if I decide I want to participate once you two have started?"

Graedon tilted his head. "As you wish."

Paige caught the flash in his eyes. Clearly, Graedon wanted the first time just to be the two of them. But if Connor decided to join in, she would never discourage him. This was for him too. Not just Graedon. Not just her.

Instead of heading to the chair, Connor moved closer to the two of them. "I want to at least help the two of you undress."

"Yes," Paige agreed enthusiastically. She loved when Connor took his time undressing her, exposing her body little by little, appreciating it along the way. It was one of her favorite acts of foreplay. Though, honestly, Paige never had done any foreplay that wasn't her favorite. Anything that titillated her was a winner.

Connor went behind Paige, placing his hands on her shoulders. "Ready?"

"Oh yes. Please." Her breathing shallowed as her husband ran his fingers down her arms to her waist, grasping the hem of her sweater.

Connor's gaze shifted to Graedon. "You want to help?"

"Of course."

Both her and Connor were a bunch of nerves, but this man was an enigma. His words were calm. His demeanor cool. Not a quiver to his voice. If Paige didn't know better, she'd think he was approaching this as a business transaction. But she had no doubt his passion ran high, that it was molten like lava. She just experienced it downstairs.

Within seconds, she once again found herself sandwiched between the two men. Graedon in front, Connor behind. Both held the bottom edge of her sweater and slowly rolled it up over her breasts and her head. Connor threw it somewhere behind him, but Paige's eyes never left Graedon. His heated gaze roamed over the flesh that overflowed from her bra. She hoped he was making plans on what he intended to do with and to her breasts. Her nipples pebbled in anticipation.

Connor slid his fingers under the clasp and released the

weight the silky fabric held up. The black bra fell forward and slipped down her arms.

"So perfect," Graedon whispered.

Paige wanted him to touch her. But he didn't. He only caressed her with his eyes. Without even a touch, the man created a pool of wetness between her legs.

Graedon reached out to unsnap and unzip her jeans, while Connor went to his knees behind her, stroking around her ankles and up her calves until the denim got too snug for him to continue. He pulled his hands out from her pant legs and explored his way up over the top of the jeans until he had a grip on the waistband. With Graedon holding the front, Connor holding the back, they peeled the curve-fitting jeans over her hips and down her thighs until she was free.

They left her panties on and Connor, once again on his knees, started at her feet, licking his way up her leg until he reached the bottom of her black lacy boy shorts. Taking Connor's cue, Graedon also dropped to his knees at her feet, kissing her lower belly and circling her navel with his tongue before working his way to the top elastic band. Connor hooked his fingers in the back, Graedon worked fingers into the front, and they slipped her panties down slowly, their mouths following the panties' path. When Graedon's mouth was directly over her pubis bone, Paige grabbed onto his broad shoulders, trying desperately to stay on her feet. His tongue stroked the narrow, neat strip of hair she'd left, making her body clench as his hot breath washed over her most sensitive area.

Connor scraped his teeth along her buttocks, nipping gently here and there. Not hard enough to leave marks, but hard enough to make her whimper and dig her nails into Graedon's skin through the sweater. Her husband licked up the crease of her ass and sucked the skin at the small of her back.

They slid her panties down her thighs, and they dropped at her feet. She kicked them off so she could separate her legs as much as possible, giving Graedon room to slip two fingers along her wet, swollen lips to expose her clit. His mouth found it, sucking, licking, and flicking until she cried out and she couldn't hold on any longer.

"Easy, babe," Connor murmured, helping to support her.

She curled her fingers tighter in Graedon's sweater, helplessly tugging at it, wanting him to be as naked as she was.

After a few more strokes of his tongue, he sat back on his heels and gazed up at her, his dark lips glistening with signs of her arousal. Then he stood, kicked off his shoes, and grabbed the bottom of his sweater, ready to pull it over his head.

"No." She stopped him with a shaky voice. "No, let us."

He dropped his hands to his sides and smiled at her. "Whatever you want."

With a last kiss to the center of her back, Connor moved behind Graedon. He and Paige repeated to him what the men had done to her. They stripped him, slowly exposing his dark, smooth skin. His tight, almost black nipples, and...

Paige sucked in a breath and ran a finger gently over a long scar that ran between his heavy pec muscles. The scar was old and thick, but still pinker than the rest of his skin. She met his eyes, questioning.

Graedon's nostrils flared slightly, and he gave a quick shake of his head. Now was not the time.

Paige leaned closer to kiss along the puckered scar line then she licked his nipples, flicking each tip with her tongue.

The man had *the V*. The developed line of muscle that ran from his outer abs to point to secrets below. Secrets Paige wanted to discover.

She peeked at Connor. He'd noticed too.

Though Connor was very fit, he didn't have that scrumptious V. And Paige hoped he wouldn't feel self-conscious next to Graedon.

But by the look on Connor's face, he appeared captivated by it too.

Graedon shoved his fingers into her long hair, gripping tight enough to pull her scalp painfully. But it felt so good. So right.

He pulled her head back and kissed along her neck as Connor worked Graedon's jeans open, running a hand over the bulge in his boxer briefs. "Fuck," Connor said, as he discovered how big the other man was. He made quick work of removing Graedon's jeans, briefs, and socks until the man stood before him nude.

Graedon's heavy cock fell against Paige's belly. Between the heat and size of him as well as his mouth on her skin, she cried out in sheer desperate need.

Connor came around the larger man to kiss Paige's shoulder before heading to the chair in the corner. He sprawled in the seat, his legs spread wide, and he unfastened his own jeans, pushing them down enough to be able to slide his hand inside.

Paige bit back a squeal as Graedon swung her into his arms. She felt tiny, like a doll, as his muscles bunched and tightened around her. He placed her at the edge of the mattress, pushing her upper body flat, pulling her ass to the edge, before going to his knees between her thighs. He settled her feet on his shoulders and dove in.

Literally.

Paige arched her back, her mouth gaping, as his lips moved along her pussy and his tongue invaded her. He sucked in her folds, her clit, the tender skin in the crease of her thigh. He bit her swollen flesh before plunging two fingers deep inside her. She pushed her hips off the bed, mashing herself against his mouth as he worked her. Oh, did he work her into a frenzy. Mindless, she rocked her head back and forth, as he sucked her clit hard and plunged his large fingers in and out of her until...

"Fuck!" she screamed at the ceiling. She forced her eyes open to watch his head move between her legs—faster, harder—and she wailed uncontrollably, her eyes rolling back as the waves of climax crashed through her. She clamped her thighs around his head, her clit too sensitive to continue, but he was relentless, not even pausing for her to enjoy the first orgasm before he wrenched another one from deep inside her. Her toes curled, and she slammed her palms against the mattress, screaming at him to stop. It was too much, too fast. And then suddenly…

He was gone.

She closed her eyes, willing her heart to stop pounding out of her chest, to stop the trembling in her legs, for her body to accept the oxygen she inhaled at a rapid pace.

He returned quickly, his hands on her ribs, pushing her up along the bed. The mattress dipped under his weight, and without a pause, his body covered hers completely, his hips between her thighs. He pinned her arms above her head by the wrists with one of his broad hands. He took one nipple into his mouth, swirling his tongue around the edge and then the hard center. His trimmed goatee roughly brushed the delicate skin of her breast.

He sucked the nipple deep, pulling as much flesh into his mouth as possible. His other hand clasped her other breast, his finger and thumb pinching and twisting the hard peak not so gently.

There was nothing refined about this man in bed. His elegant demeanor had disappeared, and the man who appeared in his place was rough, animalistic. Nothing held him back.

He moved to her mouth, sucking on her lower lip, then stroking it with his tongue. "Can you taste yourself?"

Paige released a shaky breath. "Yes."

"I made you come twice with my mouth. How many times can I make you come with my cock?"

Something about the words *come* and *cock* coming out of his mouth, made her groan. "Are you going to fuck me?"

"Yes."

"Hard?"

"So fucking hard," he said roughly in his deep-timbre voice.

His dirty words thrilled her, and she found herself desperate to kiss his filthy mouth. She willed him to say fuck again. To tell her how long he would fuck her. How deep he would fuck her. Fuck. Fuck. *Fuck.* "You're going to make me come?" she asked.

Graedon must have realized the game she was playing, and with a smile against her skin, he said, "I'm going to bang you so hard with my fucking cock, you are going to scream when you come. And then I'm going to fuck you all over again. Until you soak me."

Paige shuddered. When he released her arms, she grabbed his biceps and squirmed underneath him.

On his right bicep, she felt another thick scar under her fingertips, distracting her for a second. But his quick movement to settle his cock against her swollen, ready lips made her forget everything but what he was about to do. He was already encased in latex, and Paige realized that was why he had momentarily disappeared earlier. Her body tensed as he pressed forward, ready for the pressure of accommodating a man of his size.

"Relax," he whispered, his face inches above hers. "I'll go slow."

She didn't want him to go slow. She wanted him now. Deep inside her.

But he was right, even if taking his time might be her complete undoing.

He held her face in his hands, pinning his gaze to hers. She'd never seen such an intense look before, causing her to spook a little bit. But it also made her tremor in anticipation. Little by little, he pushed his hips forward, his mouth open, but not quite touching hers. He inhaled her breath; she inhaled his. In and out. In and out. And it was driving her crazy.

He lied about taking it slow. He took her. Her mouth, her slick center. Hard. Kissing her fiercely, fucking her ferociously, stretching her to the breaking point. The heavy muscles of his body working, pumping, holding her in place as she cried into his mouth.

Not to stop. No.

But to continue.

He was so fucking strong. He seized control of her body by using his against her.

She wrapped her legs around his thick thighs, feeling the corded muscles expand and contract with each thrust. When she reached to grab his waist, he took her hands and pinned them to the bed, holding her.

This man was all about control. All about what was *his*.

And in that moment, he had made her his conquest. He occupied her mouth and her body completely. Each pump of his hips, making her wetter, stretching her to accommodate his girth.

It felt so fucking exhilarating.

He clamped his mouth to the base of her throat and sucked her skin until it was tender. Again and again, he took her. Sweat sheened their bodies; their cries, moans, and groans echoed each other.

He grabbed the curved flesh of her breast between his teeth, nipping her skin until he found the nipple, peaked, puckered, and waiting. The pull of his mouth, the graze of his teeth brought her to the verge of climax.

He fucked her fast and furious, the pleasure building at her center until it exploded outward from her core. The waves of orgasm rocked through her, causing her to dig her toes into his calves and her breath to hitch until it burst from her in a wail.

Graedon grunted when she slammed her pelvis into his, trying to prolong the orgasm. "More?" The question didn't sound so cool and calm now. It was raw, feral.

"Yes," she hissed.

He slowed his thrust, released her hands, and slid his palms under her ass, lifting her hips. Then he did something with his motion that drove her almost insane. With every roll of his hips, his cock stroked her spot, that pleasurable magic target which made her wetter, made her body clench harder around him while trying to pull him deeper. But it was impossible. He completely filled her; there was nowhere else to go.

The rock of his hips put pressure on her clit, and she shattered again. Her mouth opened but no sound escaped. Her head rocked back, and her fingernails dug into his solid arms leaving tiny half-moon indentations.

His breath hitched, and his body faltered for a moment, but within seconds, he found a completely new rhythm. Pushing himself up straighter, he grabbed both sides of her hips and plunged into her at a new angle. She thrashed against him uncontrollably, her inner walls constricting around him. The last climax was short but deep and intense.

His endurance was amazing. Besides the sheen of his skin, there was no indication of him working hard. He wasn't out of breath; he wasn't slowing because he got tired. He kept running like a machine. His cock a well-oiled piston.

Who had that type of control? Was it mind over matter?

But Paige could only take so much. She was about to disintegrate into dust. She felt the pull of exhaustion, her multiple orgasms draining her.

"Are you done?" he asked roughly and placed a kiss between her breasts.

"Toast," she said in a broken sigh.

He gave her a satisfied smile and moved his hands back up to cup her cheeks, holding her head still, forcing her to meet his gaze. When he shuddered, his eyes closed for a brief moment, his smile wavered, and his fingers pressed harder into her face.

Then he stilled, his breathing heavy and quick.

He dropped his forehead to hers. "I hope you found that satisfactory." Before she could even process what he said, he slipped out of her and off the bed. He went into the master bathroom and shut the door behind him.

Boneless and completely depleted, she was incapable of movement. She didn't even have the energy to slide her legs shut.

Even though he had left her, she could still feel his fullness, the stretch of him. And she would probably feel it for at least a day.

She was wrecked.

She smiled up at the ceiling.

And then she remembered Connor. He hadn't joined them. He hadn't stopped them. He hadn't said a word.

She dug up enough energy to turn her head toward the chair.

Connor appeared just as totaled as her and he hadn't even been in the bed. His jeans gaped open, his hands still, his hair disheveled, and his shirt wrinkled with a dark stain along the bottom. His eyes were hooded when he met her gaze, his voice breathless. "Holy fuck."

Paige gave him a small smile. "Yeah, holy fuck."

***

The three of them sat at the head of the bed. Connor just in his jeans since his shirt was in the laundry. Graedon, also shirtless, wore black silk pajama bottoms. And Paige had said "fuck it" and only dragged on her boy short panties.

At this point, she didn't have the energy to worry about sitting almost completely naked on their new lover's bed while they munched on grapes, apple slices, cheese, and crackers. Of course, those were the kind of snacks he kept in the house. She would have been surprised if he came back into the bedroom with a bag of corn chips. She doubted that bad-assed body of his was fueled on junk food.

Connor and Graedon took turns feeding her grapes as she lounged between them and against the pillows.

"When do I get fed chocolate-covered strawberries? Oh, or cherries. Where are the concubines with the palm frond fans?"

"Do you think you're going to be spoiled like this every time?" Connor asked.

"I expect it."

Connor snorted, and she couldn't hold her laughter. Though she and Connor knew when each was kidding with the other, Graedon hadn't picked up on the ball-busting sense of humor they had.

"A woman should always be spoiled. Kept like a queen. Keep her happy, and she has no reason to stray."

Well then. First of all, Graedon using a word like "kept" worried her. She frowned as he placed a slice of apple to her lips. She turned her head to reject it, and he placed it back on the plate.

"I don't want to be *kept* like a queen."

"Treated like a queen, then. If that's better suited."

Sure, but he had said *kept.*

"A woman should also spoil her man. Or men, in this case. It's a two-way street," Paige stated.

"That it is," he answered her, his voice deep and delicious.

She grabbed a cracker off of the plate and dipped it in the soft, melty brie cheese. She popped it in her mouth and closed her eyes with the sheer richness of it. "This shit is the bomb. I need to buy some of this."

"I buy it at a specialty store. I'll get you some next time I go."

Of course, he bought it at a specialty store. Why would he buy cheese at the grocery store like the rest of the "normal folk?" This got her wondering about his past and if he had come from an upper-class family. Had he gone to an expensive private school? An Ivy League college? But if so, why did he end up as a football player on the Boston Bulldogs? Why play a game that beats the hell out of your body, if you had the brains to sit behind a desk and make a fortune? No concussions. No bruises. No ice baths and deep tissue massages to work out all the knots and tightness after a brutal game.

And that scar on his chest…

The raised skin on his right bicep definitely wasn't a scar exactly. It had a specific shape, and she recognized it as a brand. Who would brand themselves? That had to be torture. She'd seen quite a few black players in the NFL with the symbols of their college fraternities. Though neither Ty, Cole, nor Renny had one. The brand made fraternity members brothers for life, she guessed.

They had so much to learn about this new man in their bed—or tonight, technically *his* bed—and she wanted to find out what made him into the man he was and what made him tick.

She could do an inquisition and bombard him with questions, or she could pull the information out slowly as they went along. She guessed it would depend on how much he minded giving up intel on himself. After her questioning when he visited the sod farm the other day, she realized he wasn't the type to be real chatty about his personal background. "Tell me about the scar."

Unconsciously, he ran his finger down it and his brows pinned together.

Connor leaned forward and asked, "Can I touch it?"

Graedon studied him for a moment before nodding. For a second, it had actually looked like he might say no.

Connor reached over Paige to run his fingers from the ragged edge that began at the bottom of his throat all the way to where it ended mid-stomach.

Graedon grew very still as he allowed Connor to touch him.

"It's wicked. Heart surgery?" Connor inquired, moving his hand back over the other man's heart and leaving it there. Graedon's nostrils flared slightly.

Paige didn't know if it was from the question or Connor's touch. She dropped her gaze to his lap, and Graedon's erection tented the black silk he wore. Well, there was the answer.

Graedon's gaze moved from Connor's arm to Paige's face, and there was a question in his eyes.

Was he asking her permission if he could touch her husband? She gave him a slight nod, and Graedon leaned over, reaching out to grab the back of Connor's head, pulling him closer. Connor didn't resist as Graedon brought their lips together, sealing his mouth over Connor's.

The two men kissing over her was the hottest shit she'd ever seen. Heat immediately pooled in her core. She wondered whose tongue was in whose mouth as she watched their lips move, their jaws shift, and their eyes close.

Paige blew out a breath and leaned back further against the headboard so she could see more of them, of what they were doing. She wanted to reach out but was afraid she'd disrupt their actions. From the bulge she could see under Connor's jeans, they had made the right decision. The men wanted each other. Which was good, because she wanted them both as well.

Connor dropped his hand from Graedon's heart to his erection, smoothing his fingers over the silk of the other man's pajama pants. Before she could move the plate of food out of the way, Connor rose to his knees and climbed over Paige, not even breaking the kiss.

Graedon's long, dark fingers entwined in Connor's dirty blond hair as he assisted Connor to get closer.

When Paige could finally grab the plate, she put it on the nightstand, then shifted to give Connor more room. But he didn't settle between her and Graedon. Instead, he moved until he was lying between Graedon's legs. One of them groaned as Graedon spread his thighs wider to accommodate Connor's large body.

Connor finally broke the kiss, his lips shiny and swollen, his eyes glazed. "I want to try—"

"This?" Graedon asked him, his eyes dark, as he shoved the elastic waistband of his pants down enough for his erection to escape. The head was already slick with precum.

Paige felt a pull of envy since Connor would be the first to taste Graedon.

Connor palmed the hard length, and though Connor's hands were not small, Graedon's cock still couldn't be contained within Connor's grip. Connor slid down enough to drop his head until only a hair's breadth was between his mouth and the larger man's cock.

Paige chewed at her bottom lip. Connor had never taken another man in his mouth. And for the first to be someone of Graedon's size worried her. She wanted this to be a memorable experience, not a disaster.

Connor reached his tongue out to lick the slickness off the head. Then without hesitation, he wrapped his lips around the shaft, mimicking movements he probably learned from Paige doing the same to him.

Paige didn't want to think how weird her thoughts were, but she felt proud of her husband sucking their new lover's cock like a champ. She turned her eyes up to Graedon's face. She blinked.

He stared at her, a slight grimace on his face as Connor's head bobbed up and down. Paige was so fucking wet, and it only got worse with the realization of Graedon watching her. He seemed to be studying her reactions.

Graedon left one hand entwined in Connor's hair and reached out his other, snagging her long hair and bringing her to him. He captured her lips, kissing her fiercely.

She groaned into his mouth and reached her hand out blindly until she found Connor's head, she entangled her fingers in his hair, next to Graedon's. Feeling the rise and fall of his head under her hand as she kissed Graedon made her squeeze her thighs together. She wanted to push Connor out of the way and mount Graedon where he sat until she got off a quick one. Something to take off the edge.

At the same time, Connor's head slowed, the noises in his throat got quiet, and Graedon pulled away just enough from Paige to be able to grit his teeth and close his eyes. "Let me go unless you want me to come in your mouth." The words were raw, his fingers digging harder into Paige's hair as he tensed.

Connor didn't move away. Instead, he stilled as Graedon's hips lifted slightly, a grunt escaping his lips.

Paige's pussy was soaked, and her muscles twinged at the

sounds, the sight, and everything surrounding Graedon's release and Connor's acceptance.

After a moment, Connor lifted his head and looked at her.

Graedon reached down and grabbed his biceps pulling him up to lay a solid kiss on Connor's mouth.

As soon as Connor was free, Paige did the same, kissing her husband and whispering, "That was so hot, baby."

Graedon leaned back against the headboard, his eyes hooded, and his body relaxed as he stroked Connor's back with one hand and, after wrapping an arm around Paige, he trailed his fingers up and down her ribs.

She tucked her legs and curled tighter against him. She brushed an unruly lock of hair off of Connor's forehead as he laid it on Graedon's thigh.

Paige smiled at the both of them. "I guess I'm not going to be the only one spoiled."

CHAPTER 4

Leaving Graedon's bed the other night had been the hardest thing they'd had to do in a while. Reluctantly, Connor had peeled himself away from the new man in his life to head home with his wife.

That in itself did not sound normal. He laughed and shook his head. But he was happy the evening had gone so well. He'd had been nervous before they went over to Graedon's house, but when they'd left, he'd been relaxed. Sleepy even. And he couldn't wait to get together with him again. He wanted to explore so much more with this new relationship. It was obvious Paige felt the same.

Watching Graedon take control of his wife in bed, watching her shatter into pieces as she orgasmed over and over, had driven him over the edge too. He had been caught with his pants down. Literally.

Connor smiled to himself. Even though he'd been bi-curious for as long as he could remember, he never did anything about it —besides flirt with his brother-in-law, Ty. So he wasn't sure, when it came down to it, if he would even enjoy having sexual contact with another man. Yes, he'd been attracted to other men, but actually giving a blowjob, or eventually having sex with one, had been questionable.

However, it ended up feeling right, only natural, when he took Graedon into his mouth and ultimately swallowed the man's release. It hadn't bothered him one bit, and he actually enjoyed it. He also felt proud that he hadn't gagged once.

"What are you smiling about?" Paige smacked him on the ass as she moved by him.

"The other night."

Paige froze mid-step and turned toward him. "So, we're good, right?"

"Good? Me and you? Of course."

"Well, that too. But I'm really asking if you think he's the right one."

"I think so. Though, it was only one evening," he answered.

"You never asked me how I felt about the whole thing."

"Paige. I didn't have to. I saw everything that happened. There was nothing but pleasure on your face during and satisfaction after."

Not to mention, the excitement of anticipation beforehand.

He loved that his wife was passionate enough to go on this journey with him. Her loving sex definitely helped. He wasn't worried about Paige and Graedon getting together when he was out of town because their relationship was solid. They were still as sexually attracted to each other now as when they met. He was truly a lucky man.

His wife moved around the kitchen while preparing breakfast and he watched her. Her ass, the bounce of her breasts, the swing of her hips, and the toss of her head. It made him want to take her right there on the counter. Or the floor. Or the kitchen table.

"What's your plans for today?" she asked, her back still to him.

Connor moved up behind her and wrapped his arms around her, placing a kiss on her bare shoulder. He loved when she wore old, worn tank tops with no bra. Her nipples pressed through the thin fabric. He tweaked one hard. "First, I may have to bend you over and fuck you."

She turned her head and grinned at him. "That will take all of five minutes. Then what?"

This time Connor spanked her on the ass, causing her to jump and squeal before laughing. She pushed her hips back against him playfully.

"I don't know. You want to do something?" he asked.

"Call Graedon and have copious amounts of sex?"

"Sure. But I think we need to get together with him again and find out more about him first. Don't you?"

"We can do that between rounds of sweaty sex," she suggested, laughter in her voice.

"I'd rather have you to myself this morning." He pushed her tank top up and over her breasts, kneading the soft flesh. "Turn the stove off."

She did as he suggested and then turned in his arms to face him.

Connor brushed his hard-on against her. "That's not morning wood, babe. That's all you," he told her.

"Hmm. That's what all the men say."

"All the men. Right. Just one. Well, and now Graedon." He steered her to the counter island and cleared it with his arm before lifting her enough to settle her ass on it. "Maybe I should've taken your pants off first," he said.

Hooking her fingers into the waistband of her yoga pants, she wiggled out of them. She threw them on his head, laughing. "There." Since she always went commando under her yoga pants, she had nothing else to do but spread her knees to give him full access. She gave him a come-hither smile and leaned back on her elbows. "What are you waiting for?"

His wife wore only the white tank, the dark pink color of her nipples visible through the fabric—a sight that never tired him. She remained as sexy as the day he saw her at the stadium she'd been working at. She had been dirty, sweaty, and like a pissed off hellcat since her and Logan had been stuck doing all the sod-laying. But, damn, the moment he saw her, he knew she was the one.

"You're beautiful, babe," he murmured against her lips. He kissed her lips, her chin, then down her neck. Pushing the tank top up over her breasts once more, he kissed each one gently. "You liked it rough with Graedon, didn't you?"

"Yes," she hissed, curling her fingers around his head and pulling him closer.

"You want me to be more like that?"

"Connor, I want you to be you."

He shucked the long shorts he wore and ripped down his boxer briefs. His erection poked her inner thigh as he shifted into place until he could feel her heat and slick arousal. "Should I feel guilty that I'm fucking my own wife without Graedon here?"

"Never," she murmured.

He pushed inside her slowly, savoring the warm tightness surrounding him, a wet fist clenched snugly around his length. Every time Connor was inside his wife, he felt like he was home. With a grunt, he settled fully inside her, not moving for a moment. They had all the time in the world this morning since they had no plans. He wanted to enjoy every second of being a part of Paige.

When she wiggled impatiently beneath him, he began to move. Her legs wrapped around his waist as she tried to pull him closer, deeper.

"Patience, Paige. There's no rush." He kissed down her belly.

"Shut up and fuck me."

She always made him laugh and he did so now. Paige never minced words. He tightened his fingers around her hips and held her in place when he pounded her, her body jerking with each hard thrust.

Her cell phone vibrated across the counter, then again, moving closer to where they were. It bumped against Paige's ribcage and went silent.

Connor ignored it, gritting his teeth as he gave his wife one hundred percent of his attention. His hair fell across his forehead as he picked up the pace, making the small of her back bow. They knew each other inside and out; he knew what she liked and what she needed to make her come. He tilted his hips slightly and dug his fingers deeper into her flesh. He dropped his head to her chest and squeezed his eyes shut. The sounds coming out of Paige's mouth were about to be his undoing. She clamped down tighter. Her legs, her arms, her pussy, until he couldn't hold on any longer.

Luckily, Paige tensed and cried out, "I'm coming," just as he lost himself deep within her. He stilled, and her body went boneless underneath him. She released a long sigh.

"I'll have that type of breakfast any day of the week," he murmured against her heated skin.

"Mmm, yeah. I agree." She wiped a hand across her forehead, whisking away the sweat. She was in no rush to move, nor was he.

Then her phone buzzed again, against her side. She cursed and grabbed it, glancing at the screen. "Fuck," Paige whispered as she read the text. She handed him the phone.

Graedon. He was inviting them on his boat for the day since it was an unusually warm spring day.

"It's like he knew what we were doing." Connor suddenly felt guilty, even though he knew the thought was ridiculous. He moved away from Paige, grabbing some wet paper towels to clean himself up with, handing her a handful also.

"That's crazy," Paige said, sliding off the counter to pull her yoga pants back on.

"Right?"

"Disinfect the counter while I finish making breakfast."

"I'm hungrier now than ever," he said.

Paige glanced at the clock on the stove. "See? Five minutes."

"Funny." Actually, it wasn't. Especially, since another man was in the picture who appeared to have better control than he did.

Paige patted his arm as he tugged on his shorts. "It's not a competition, honey. I'm just busting your balls."

"I know." But he didn't feel any better about it. They couldn't ignore Graedon's text, though. "Do you want to go?"

"It's Saturday. You're in town. We have no plans." She peeked out of the window over the sink. "It looks like it's going to be a beautiful day. I say yes."

"You want to text him back?"

Before Paige could answer, the phone vibrated again. She looked at the caller ID and swiped her finger across the screen. "Hey, I was just about to text you back."

Connor watched a range of emotions cross his wife's face as she spoke to Graedon. He got impatient listening to the one-sided conversation. He mouthed *"speaker phone"* to her and she obliged.

Graedon's deep, rich voice came through the little speaker giving her an address where to meet him.

"Do you want us to bring anything?" Paige asked.

"Just yourselves. I've got everything else covered. Don't bother with bathing suits either. The water is too cold."

Last thing Connor needed was to get into cold water and shrivel up to a peanut next to the definitely larger man. He already didn't feel thrilled with his lack of endurance this morning.

"Okay, what time do you want us there?"

"One. I'll meet you in the parking lot of the yacht club and escort you down to the dock since you need a key card to access it."

Paige eyeballed him to see if he was thinking the same thing. Yacht club. Key card. He probably didn't have a little dinghy.

"Sounds good. We'll be there at one."

"Don't let her be late, Connor," came Graedon's warning from the phone.

See? He knew somehow that they'd just had sex. Paige hadn't told him either since Connor had been standing next to her in the kitchen.

"I'm never late," Paige complained.

"Connor?"

He chuckled. "We'll be there on time. I promise."

Graedon disconnected the phone without so much as a goodbye.

***

Paige sat at the bow of the boat, her hair blowing behind her as she lifted her face to the sun. Even though it felt warmer than the usual spring day, the breeze out on the lake was a bit cooler. But it still felt good. The bitter cold of winter was long gone and the hot humid days were around the corner. She hoped their new lover would take them out on the boat again when it was warm enough to swim.

The size of the boat was impressive even though it wasn't quite a yacht. It was large enough to haul quite a bunch of people and it had a master stateroom—as Graedon called the bedroom, a galley kitchen, and a full bathroom or head, below. All perfectly clean and every stainless-steel surface shined. He seemed very particular with his possessions.

She felt certain it applied to his human "possessions" also.

While she enjoyed the view as he skippered the boat around the lake, Connor was back at the wheel with Graedon as he taught him the ins and outs of boating.

Paige decided to stay away while the men took the time to bond.

Graedon had been pleased to see them arrive with a couple minutes to spare and greeted them with a large smile. He kissed her directly on the lips, lingering longer than a kiss in a normal greeting. Then he shook Connor's hand. She guessed it would have been weird if he also had kissed Connor hello.

What was the protocol to greet another male lover, especially after Connor had his mouth around Graedon's cock and had swallowed the man's load?

Is there some sort of after-blowjob etiquette?

Paige laughed into the wind, brushing the hair out of her face. When the day ended, it would be full of knots, but she didn't care. She felt completely relaxed and stress-free. She took a deep breath to inhale the fresh, cool air.

Graedon approached her along the port side of the boat. The nautical term was the very first thing Graedon had taught them. The port side was left, the starboard right, the bow the front, the stern the back. If that was all she had to learn today, she was fine with it. Let the men do their manly thing.

She turned her head, her hair whipping her face sharply, to watch him move with ease along the walkway to the bow, even though the water was a little choppy.

He wore another snug long-sleeve Henley, this time a shade of pink, salmon maybe, with the sleeves pushed halfway up his muscular arms. It highlighted the dark tone of his skin, pulling out the eggplant undertones. Yes, he didn't seem a man worried about being judged for wearing pink. More men would wear the color if they looked as good as he did.

His thick, muscular legs were encased in black jeans and his feet bare. He settled next to her on the raised center of the bow, nudging her over with his hip.

"Shouldn't you be driving this thing?" she asked, surprised and a little worried he left her husband in charge.

"Connor has it."

"Really? You sure you want him in control of this—what, a hundred grand, at least—boat? I hope you have insurance."

Graedon chuckled, his lips broadening enough to show his

bright white teeth. "He'll be fine. We're in deep open water. Nothing to hit but maybe another boat."

"Oh, that's reassuring."

Graedon reached out to her, tucking a wild strand of hair behind her ear. It didn't stay there very long. "Don't bite your lip. Connor and I should be the only ones biting it."

Paige hadn't even realized she'd been doing it. Bad habit. She stopped abruptly.

"That's better. You have beautifully curved lips made to pleasure a man."

She smiled at him. "Like Connor did to you?"

He didn't answer for a moment but instead looked away out over the water. Was he ashamed of liking men? He hadn't really discussed it. Which seemed sort of odd. No. Can't be. This man couldn't be embarrassed at anything he did. He would own every decision he made.

He finally looked back at her and ran his thumb over her lip. "I look forward to you doing what he did. Perhaps when we stop at one of the secluded coves and anchor."

She shivered with anticipation. "Everything he did to you he learned from me, I'll have you know. Don't forget, you are the first man he's been with."

"I haven't forgotten." He grabbed the back of her neck and tilted her head back enough to stare intently into her eyes. "Why didn't you answer the first time I called this morning?"

"I was making breakfast."

His fingers dug firmly into her skin. "That all?"

Paige's breath quickened. "No."

"Was he fucking you?"

Her heart thudded. "Yes."

"Where?"

"In the kitchen."

"Where?"

"On the island." Suddenly, she imagined Graedon taking her

on the counter, his muscles flexing as he pumped into her, bringing her to orgasm.

"Did you come?"

"Yes," she hissed.

"How many times?"

"Once."

Graedon leaned in and softly brushed her lips with his. "I would've made you come at least twice." He released her abruptly.

She swallowed hard, gathering her wits. "As I had to remind Connor, this isn't a competition. It won't work if you two make it into one."

"That is correct. However, the agreement was as long as I'm in town, I must be included. When Connor is in town, he must be."

Paige pinned her lips together. "Yes, I agree. But it was spur of the moment."

"So if I took you here on the bow of the boat, right now, that would be fine with Connor?"

"I don't know."

"Should I go ask him?"

Paige pinned her eyebrows together. "No."

"So, you understand my dilemma?"

"Yes."

"He has access to you more since you live together. This may be a problem."

The last thing Paige wanted to do was move in with a man they just met. She also knew Connor would not agree to that either. But she understood where he was coming from. She knew from Logan's relationship that everything had to be equal and out in the open. Otherwise, Logan, Ty, and Quinn's relationship would have failed by now. They knew how to balance everything.

She may have to have a conversation with her brother.

No. Yuck.

Maybe Quinn. Yes, Quinn made more sense. Paige was close enough to her sister-in-law to ask her those types of questions.

"What do you suggest?" she asked the man who studied her face intently. She schooled her expression.

"I'll give it some thought."

You do that.

"Excuse me, while I go take over the helm. I'll take us to a cove where we can enjoy some of the lunch I had specially made for us." He leaned over and gave her a deeper kiss this time, his tongue sliding along her lips before he broke away and stood up with a snap of his spine. "Relax and enjoy the ride. We should be at our destination in about fifteen minutes."

Aye, aye, Captain. She resisted the urge to salute him. "Graedon," she called out as he started to work his way back to the stern.

He turned slightly toward her.

"Thank you for this. For today."

Graedon tilted his head in acknowledgment. "The day isn't over yet." He continued on, leaving her alone at the bow.

No, the day certainly wasn't over yet. Paige wondered what else he had planned.

CHAPTER 5

Grae sipped at the Cristal Champagne he had poured, the red raspberries at the bottom of the flute causing bubbles to float up the delicate glass. The three of them sat relaxed at the open stern of the boat, content after filling themselves with the prepared lunch he brought with him.

He loved this boat, but he didn't use it nearly enough. However, it had been the perfect excuse to get together with Paige and Connor. Usually, he went out in it by himself to escape work. Occasionally, he anchored in a cove and slept overnight in the cabin. Something about being on the water gave him the best sleep. Sometimes, he just needed that, to sleep like the dead.

Ever since meeting the married couple, he'd had trouble sleeping. Today his intention was just a day trip unless he dropped them off and came back out on his own. A possibility he may have to consider.

He also needed to contemplate Connor and Paige's impulsive sex since they lived together. One thing he had problems with in his past triad was he'd become the third wheel. He didn't want that to happen again.

From the get-go, Paige had drawn him in hard and fast. After seeing her across the room the night of Ty's birthday party, he hadn't stopped thinking about her since. An obsession. He'd never been one to fixate on people or things. So this disturbed him. It had, honestly, caught him off guard.

Connor being part of the package, though, was fine with him. The younger man was attractive and intelligent. But the real reason he could deal with Connor was the man belonged to Paige.

When he noticed Paige staring at him that night, things couldn't have been made easier for him. Little did he know, at the time, Paige was Logan's sister. So, he had to proceed carefully. Last thing he wanted was a pissed off brother, not to mention friend, gunning for him. He didn't have a lot of personal acquaintances, so the ones he had, he valued and wanted to retain.

The other night went better than he'd planned. He made Paige his and luckily, Connor didn't get spooked about being with another man. Which had been Grae's biggest concern. If Connor backed out, he would have to let his plans with Paige go. That would be very unfortunate.

Especially since he had a hard time letting go of what was his. Or what *should* be his.

But if he had to, he could do it. Though, he wouldn't be pleased with the outcome, of course.

Now the couple had their feet kicked up, full stomachs, sipping on Champagne as the anchored boat floated calmly in the cove. He knew this inlet well since it was one of his favorite sleeping spots.

Paige had her head tilted back against the bench seat, her eyes closed, letting the sun warm her face. Connor had downed half of his flute of bubbly and sat staring at him.

Grae pretended not to notice. Let the man stare. He wanted Paige's husband to feel completely comfortable with him.

However, he still needed to address the dilemma of Connor being able to have Paige whenever and wherever he wanted to. He could have them move temporarily into his home, but they might not agree to that. Or move into their home? Grae wasn't sure where they lived, or if their house was even large enough to accommodate all of them.

Grae was used to making important decisions without having to consult anyone else. The Bulldogs' owners and coaches trusted his decisions completely. He knew talent when he saw it, and he also had that gut instinct important in his field. That great instinct had given him promotion after promotion until he ended up in charge of the whole college recruiting department for the team. His subordinates came to *him* for advice and the final approval of recruiting a college player. Over the years, he'd built a strong team of recruiters and supporting personnel. He had no problems weeding out the weak. In business and in his personal life. Even so, he didn't think the couple would welcome him solely making the decision on where they lived. Even if it was only temporary.

He finally met Connor's gaze.

"About this morning..." Connor began.

Grae waved a hand, acting as if it had been nothing. Though, it bothered him more than he wanted to admit. "I thought you understood the conditions we made." He used a softer tone than what he wanted. He saw no reason to cause hard feelings at his point.

Connor gripped the stem of his glass a little tighter. "I do. But she's my wife."

"Yes, she is." He understood where Connor was coming from because if Paige were his wife, he would feel the same way.

But she wasn't.

From his peripheral vision, Grae noticed Paige's eyes pop open and her head lift to listen.

"I'm used to having her when I want." The flare of Connor's nostrils when he spoke made Grae think the man might have difficulties sharing.

"I understand."

"I can't promise it won't happen again."

It sounded like a challenge.

Grae sat up a little straighter, the muscles around his spine stiffening. He put his flute down before it shattered in his fingers. "Then this relationship will be over before it really began. Is that what you want?"

Connor looked over at Paige, who, in turn, contemplated Grae. Most likely to see if he was serious or not.

Grae was very serious. As a heart attack. "We should have equal access to each other. At least, and most importantly, in the beginning to see whether this will work or not."

"And how do you propose this?"

He was pleased Connor seemed open to suggestions. Grae glanced at Paige. "You could move into my home for now. I have plenty of room. It would be temporary unless things…change."

Paige and Connor gave each other a look.

Connor finally replied, "I don't know."

Exactly the answer Grae expected. "It's not an easy decision, I know. But considering this is not a typical dating situation, I don't have any other recommendations. Except me moving in with the two of you. Temporarily, of course."

Connor again took a fleeting glance at his wife, as if they were communicating silently. "You seem like a man who enjoys your privacy."

"I am."

"So you wouldn't mind the three of us living together…*temporarily*?" Connor asked, his eyes narrowing.

Grae could see the suspicion in his expression and hear it in his words. "Again, it would only be temporary at this point." It was certainly too soon to make any kind of permanent decision.

"We would need to discuss this first," Paige said, not looking at Grae, but her gaze glued to Connor.

"I agree. Give us some time to think about it," Connor said, before downing the rest of his Champagne.

Grae automatically stood to refill his flute, as any good host would. "Drink your Champagne, Connor. I didn't bring you two out here just for lunch." He might as well not delay any longer. He stood in between the two reasons he'd invited them onto the boat. He wanted to test the waters again, pun intended, with the both of them. This time he intended to bring Connor in on the action from the beginning. To push the man to his limits to see if he would break at the physical contact Grae planned.

Grae sighed as he watched the man swallow the contents of his glass. Nothing like witnessing someone down expensive Champagne like it was beer.

But as Connor up-righted his now empty flute, the man gave him a heated smile.

Grae took the gesture as an acceptance. "Below deck or up here? The guests' choice."

"Below," Connor quickly answered, an edge of nervousness in his voice.

Grae reached out his hand and Connor took it, his long, strong fingers gripping Grae's tightly. There was nothing wimpy about Connor, and he liked that. He had a great dislike for the weak. Nervousness of the unknown, Grae could accept, but outright weakness he wouldn't tolerate.

Grae swept an arm toward the hatch to the galley. "After you." He watched Connor go down the steps and turned toward Paige. He offered a hand to her. "Paige."

Paige accepted it, letting Grae pull her to her feet and into his arms. He crushed his lips to hers for a few seconds, then released her to look down into her eyes. "I'm going to test your husband today to make sure this is really what he wants. Otherwise, there is no reason for us to go further."

She nodded without releasing his gaze. He liked that about her. She never seemed intimidated enough to look away. Or even pull away. She gave as good as she got. He'd always been attracted to women with backbone.

"That's fine. If he says no, though, you must stop immediately."

Grae raised his brows. "Of course." He would never not take no for an answer. He would never force himself on anyone. "And you can always say no, as well."

Paige gave him a slight smile as if there couldn't be anything he would do to her to make her say no. "And you as well."

Grae chuckled and nodded. He led her to the hatch, helping her down the steep steps. When his eyes adjusted to the dimness below, he saw Connor stepping out of the head. Grae studied the man. His dirty blond hair, with the shaggy length longer than he would prefer. The masculine features of his face. The hard line of his jaw. The breadth of the man's shoulders. Not nearly as wide as his own, but Grae had no desire to sleep with someone as bulky as himself. Connor was an attractive man, and not lacking in any way. A good complement to Paige.

Grae had been lucky to fall into this situation, but he wanted to proceed with care, making sure the failures of his last polyamory relationship did not repeat itself. He pointed toward the stateroom at the bow of the boat.

Connor followed his direction, while Paige shadowed her husband.

Grae was overcome with an intense urge to toss Paige on the bed and take her then and there. No fancy words or actions, just pure raw sex. He wanted to thrust mindlessly between her legs, feeling her hot, wet sheath grip him tightly while he fisted her long dark hair.

His cock agreed as it stiffened in his jeans. Although, that particular desire would have to wait. He needed to concentrate on Connor right now.

The stateroom was a tight fit, the bed taking up most of the narrow room. The three of them in it would be a squeeze, but then the idea was to be close to each other anyhow. Paige climbed onto the mattress to give the men room to stand in the limited floor space. But there wasn't much even so. They were close enough to feel each other's breath.

"Face the bed," he directed Connor.

He obliged without a word.

With the man's wide back to him, Grae took his time undressing him. He ran fingers through his blond tresses, down his neck, and with a painful slowness, removed Connor's long-sleeved T. The man's lean back muscles came into view as he peeled the shirt away. Grae stroked fingers over Connor's skin, down his spine, around his waist. He tossed the shirt into a built-in corner cubby and proceeded to unbutton Connor's jeans, unzipping them with great patience, feeling the man's erection beneath his fingers.

With both palms, Grae shoved the denim and boxer briefs down enough to release the man's hard length. Then with arms wrapped around Connor from behind, Grae took him into his hand. He stroked the velvet skin with such deliberateness that it would have driven him crazy if someone had been doing the same to him.

Precum beaded at Connor's opening and Grae smoothed it along the man's swollen head. Grae thrust his own hard-on against his still denim-covered ass.

To think that ass was untouched made Grae a little light-headed. He would be the first—and maybe the only—man to explore him there. In a way, it would be a privilege to be his first. *If* they got that far…

The man could always say no. And like Grae said several times, he would respect that decision without hesitation.

So far, Connor showed no signs of stopping him.

Paige had slid up the bed to lean against the hull of the boat, watching the two of them. Her eyes were hooded and dark, her lips parted slightly. Her chest rising and falling a little quicker than normal as she enjoyed the display so far.

He turned his attention back to the male in front of him.

Connor had arranged his hand over Grae's, directing Grae's

motion up and down his hard length, his hips picking up the rhythm.

Grae placed his mouth at the top of Connor's spine, sucking, licking, and nipping the smooth, flawless skin as he continued to pump Connor's cock with his palm.

Connor made a noise and thrust harder within his fingers.

Grae pulled away, not wanting him to climax so soon. He leaned back to remove his Henley and unfasten his jeans.

Connor turned to face him, his cheeks flushed, his eyes as shadowed as Paige's. "Kiss me," he said, his voice breaking.

Grae obliged by taking his mouth fiercely, forcing open Connor's lips, and exploring with his tongue. Connor groaned and his own tongue found Grae's, tangling and swirling, making Grae harder than he already was.

He found Connor attractive, yes. But his sudden increase in desire for Connor surprised him. It'd been a while since he'd been with another man. He never actively sought them. Sometimes they approached him. Grae wasn't sure what it was about him that made him seem open to male lovers. He wasn't openly gay, nor even openly bi. As Connor mentioned previously, Grae was a man who liked his privacy. Especially when it came to intimacy and who he was involved with. He also didn't take sex lightly. He was not a player and hadn't been in a while. He'd grown tired of the lifestyle of his youth. He'd found it unfulfilling in so many ways.

He preferred a meaningful relationship. He enjoyed learning the ins and outs of another lover.

Like Paige.

And Connor.

The man in his arms was now trying to remove his jeans without breaking their kiss.

Grae swallowed Connor's grunt as he succeeded in pushing his jeans and underwear to his knees, but that's where the denim decided to resist his efforts. Grae smiled, which broke their connection, and he assisted Connor to undress completely.

Connor did the same for him. And when they finally stood close, totally naked, their arousals found each other as if they were two magnets.

Grae cupped Connor's sac in his hand, stroking and squeezing gently. Connor was trimmed neatly, an effort Grae appreciated. He, too, was particular about his grooming. He gave him a slight nudge and Connor took the hint, sitting on the end of the bed, his thighs wide apart. Grae dropped to his knees between them, taking Connor in his hand, then into his mouth.

Grae looked up the line of Connor's body as he worked the erection in and out of his mouth. He wanted to watch every reaction Connor had, hear every exclamation and every sigh. Pleasing a lover was the ultimate turn-on to Grae. It made his balls tighten and his cock turn to steel.

Connor fell back onto his elbows, his head dropping back, his mouth wide open. He panted with every pass of his lips. His hips lifted slightly with each stroke of Grae's tongue. Grae grazed his teeth along the crown of Connor's cock and was satisfied to watch the other man twitch under his machinations.

Grabbing the root of Connor's erection, he made a cock ring of sorts with two fingers. He squeezed until color darkened Connor's hard flesh and then once again took him deep into his mouth.

Grae enjoyed performing fellatio on other men, but it never stopped just there. The longer he sucked Connor's length the more tempted he was to flip the man over and make him his as he'd done to Paige. But he knew the time wasn't right, not yet. Connor would need more preparation. Anal sex for the first time could be unpleasant, similar to a woman losing her virginity. Done right, it went well. Done wrong? It could turn Connor off to future endeavors.

Grae loosened his fingers so the blood flowed back into Connor's hard-on. He moved away to ask, "Have you done any anal play?"

Connor's eyes cracked open and he lifted his head to look down his body at Grae. "Yes."

"With Paige?"

"Yes."

"Did you enjoy it?"

A shudder went through Connor. "I loved it. And so did she."

Grae's gaze flicked to Paige. He must have been so intent on pleasing Connor orally that he hadn't noticed she had undressed.

Sitting back with her open knees dropped outward, one hand played with a breast, the other was buried between her thighs.

Grae couldn't help but swallow hard. He inhaled deeply, the oxygen in the tight quarters suddenly lacking. The woman would be his undoing. He wanted his face to be where her hand was. He wanted to be tasting her as she came in his mouth.

He struggled to turn his attention back to Connor. But Paige kept drawing his gaze instead. He took Connor back into his mouth and shifted enough between the man's thighs to watch Paige pleasure herself while he pleasured her husband.

The situation wasn't quite unbearable. Not yet. But it would be shortly. He was going to have to bury himself deep into one or the other soon. And since he had no lube on the boat, Connor had a reprieve.

Connor's head flopped back to the mattress as he gripped the bedding in his fingers. Grae sealed his lips tightly around the steely length and sucked hard, his cheeks hollowing.

"Fuck. Oh fuck," Connor muttered, his head rolling from side to side.

Paige didn't break eye contact with Grae as his head rose and fell. She gritted her teeth and grimaced as her hand moved frantically between her legs.

Grae could only imagine how wet and hot she was as her fingers plunged in and out between her sweet, plump pussy lips. It wouldn't be long before he was between them himself.

With a sudden bow of his spine, Connor shouted he was going

to come and Grae readied himself. Within a second, Connor's release shot deep down his throat and he swallowed it with expertise. He only released Connor's cock when it stopped pulsing and the man heaved a great sigh as his body became lifeless, sprawled at the end of the bed.

Bracing his hands on Connor's thighs, Grae pushed himself to his feet. Painfully hard, his own erection wanted some relief. The head wept with need, the end glistening.

He grabbed it and stroked once, twice, before climbing onto the bed, moving toward Paige.

She'd climaxed at the same time Connor had and she now leaned her head back against the side of the boat, her breath puffing from between her lips, her hands as motionless as Connor.

But Connor wasn't as spent as Grae thought when the man rolled to his side to watch Grae approach his wife. Tugging Paige to her knees, he moved her to the center of the bed, while Connor shifted to the side to give them room.

"I want you on your hands and knees," he told her.

Without a word, Paige complied, giving Grae access to her from behind while she faced her husband.

Grae had set her up there purposely. He wanted Connor to be able to watch both of their faces when Grae took her doggy-style.

"Have you had anal before?" Grae asked.

"Yes." Her answer was soft, but, in contrast, her body had visibly tensed.

Grae schooled the pleased look from his face. "How long ago?"

"Not since college."

He looked up at Connor in surprise.

He shrugged and said, "She's never offered."

The man waited for her to offer instead of just taking what was his? How foolish. You'd never get what you want if you don't try, Grae thought. His first rule of being successful.

He reached above him to one of the small cabinets above the

bed and pulled a condom from a box. He regretted finding no lube, which was what he had suspected, and made a mental note to make sure the boat always had a supply on board. He would not be caught unprepared again.

He held out the unopened condom to Connor. "Here, come put this on me, so I can fuck your wife."

A look crossed the other man's face, but he moved forward after a slight hesitation, to pluck the condom from Grae's fingers and rip the wrapper open. Connor's thighs brushed against Paige as he reached out to grab Grae's erection and roll the latex over his length.

Grae gritted his teeth until Connor was done. He released his breath slowly, his eyes not leaving the other man's. "I want you to watch us, but when I give you instructions, I want you to obey. Do you understand?"

Again, Connor hesitated, his lips flattening out while his fingers curled into loose fists. His chest rose and fell. Once. Twice. A third time.

"Do you understand?" Grae asked more slowly, each word precise and firm. He wanted to leave no room for Connor to get the idea he could disobey.

With a slight nod of his head, Connor said, "I understand."

The power struggle between the two men quickly dissipated as Grae turned his attention to Paige. On hands and knees, her pussy was a deep pink, and slick with excitement. Her body tremored slightly.

Grae stroked a hand along her spine, over the crease of her ass, and he parted her with two fingers. "You're so beautiful," he whispered. He glanced up. "Your wife is beautiful. She's so wet and hot, I can feel how ready she is for me to be inside her. Do you think she wants me to fuck her?"

Connor visibly swallowed, his spent cock stirring enough for Grae to see how turned on the other man was.

"Yes," he answered Grae.

Grae leaned down to nip Paige's ass. One cheek then the other. "Are you ready for me, Paige? Was me sucking your husband to completion enough foreplay for you?"

Paige did not turn to him when she answered, but remained facing Connor. "Oh yes."

He slid back enough to plunge his face against her, inhaling the scent of her arousal, tasting her need. He licked her luscious folds then sucked them, making her flesh swell even more. Swiping his thumb through her wetness, he pressed the slick digit onto her tight, puckered anus. He kissed her clit gently before going to his knees behind her.

With one hand gripping his cock, he pressed against her entrance, while his thumb worked her tight ring. He shifted until he was barely penetrating her, gripped her hip with his free hand, and thrust into her with his thumb and cock all at once.

Paige cried out, her hands sliding a little from underneath her from the power of his thrust.

The initial warmth and tightness surrounding him made him slow to a stop. As he stilled, her body adjusted to him in both entrances. Her wetness made his entry easy, her body accommodating him like she'd been made specifically for him.

His hips remained still as he worked his thumb in and out of her. "Relax. You need to relax." He knew it could be dangerous to tell a woman to relax. But in this case, it was needed. Her body fought the onslaught of his thumb inside her.

"I can't relax. It feels too good," she cried out breathlessly.

"Come, Connor. Help her." Grae glanced at the other man pressed against the hull of the boat, his eyes hooded, his hand cupping his semi-erect cock.

Within seconds, Connor moved forward on hands and knees until he was directly in front of Paige. He leaned down to take her face in his hands and he kissed her hard, his head tilting, his jaw moving as he thoroughly explored Paige's mouth and lips.

As Grae watched the two of them kiss, he began the age-old

rhythm of satisfying the woman his body was connected to. He synchronized the rhythm of both his thumb and cock, plunging in and out of her. He heard her groans mix with Connor's, both muffled by the intense kiss.

Connor released her face to grab her breasts, which swung beneath her body with each thrust.

Though Grae couldn't see what Connor was doing to her nipples, he could feel the effect. The squeeze of her walls around him, the sudden upward tilt of her pelvis to open herself to him more.

Her muscles pulsated and rippled along his length as he slammed her harder, his hips slapping the flesh of her ass. He pushed his thumb deeper. Once, twice. Then he pulled it out and replaced it with two fingers.

Her gasp was loud against Connor's lips. Connor pulled back and whispered words to her which Grae couldn't hear.

An intimacy existed between the two that Grae wanted to be a part of. Needed to be included in.

It would get there, but he needed it sooner than later.

It would come, he told himself.

Then Paige was murmuring words. The demand was repeated over and over until she shouted, her fingers gripping the bedspread tightly. Hard enough he wouldn't be surprised if she shredded it with her nails.

"Fuck me! Oh—fuck! Fuck me!"

Connor fisted his own cock as he watched his wife's unrestrained passion. Her encouragement quickened Grae's pace until he stood on the same precipice as Paige. The pull and release of her inner walls made him falter, his fingers and cock deep within her. He threw his head back and closed his eyes as her wet heat enveloped him, drew him in.

The intense ripples along his length as she climaxed was his undoing. His fingers dug into the curve of her hip as he became still, his cock pulsating his release within her. With eyes remaining closed, he sucked air deep into his lungs, his body humming from his explosive reaction. Paige's body still held him tight.

When he felt Paige's arms collapse, he opened his eyes to see her head on Connor's lap. Connor was spent, evidence of his own release across his lower abdomen.

With a groan, he disengaged from Paige, allowing her body to fall to the bed. Grae smiled when he heard a loud sigh.

Paige looked as satisfied as a kitten who drank a bowl of warm milk.

Paige curled sleepily between them, the heat from their bodies not helping her stay awake. Their low male voices soothed her like a lullaby. The men talked to each other while their fingers slowly caressed her thighs, her arms, her belly.

If she were capable of purring, she'd be doing it right now.

She hadn't been paying attention to what they were talking about. Something dull like football and other sports, or some such shit. The only reason she watched football was because her brother's business was involved in it and her brother-in-law was a retired NFL player. Whenever Connor talked about football, he insisted on addressing the difference between American and Australian football and Paige heard the same diatribe a million times before. She tuned it out and simply enjoyed their light touching.

Then every once in a while, she'd rest her eyes. Like now. Her eyelids became too heavy for her to haul them back up. But before she could drift off to la-la land, a few particular words about male body parts caught her attention. Graedon's tone had become reassuring, while Connor's a little tighter.

Paige's eyes popped open. Any sleepy thoughts quickly cleared from her mind as she listened to the two men.

"I can't," Connor said, his eyes wide.

"You will."

Graedon's commanding voice sent a thrill down her body, her nipples pebbling instantly. Which seemed to happen every time he showed his dominance.

"Impossible," Connor insisted.

It wasn't hard to figure out what they were discussing. Paige sat up, almost dislodging their hands.

"It may not be today, but soon. We'll prepare you. I promise," Grae assured Connor. "This relationship is going to be one hundred percent give and take. And that means..."

"We all give. We all take," Paige finished for him.

Both sets of eyes landed on her.

She gave them an impish smile and turned to her husband. "Are you willing to try it?"

"On Graedon? Sure."

Graedon shifted next to her as Connor purposely misunderstood her. "Um, baby...I meant the other way."

"That's what we've been talking about," Graedon told her.

"I'll tell you what. I'm willing to try. As Graedon said, he'll have to prepare me. But like you said, it's give and take. And I want to explore new things too."

"Please, the two of you may call me Grae. We've been intimate. No need to keep my name so formal."

Paige repeated his name out loud. After calling him and thinking about him as Graedon, the shortened version seemed odd. "Well?" she prompted Grae about Connor's request, nudging him gently in the ribs with her elbow.

Grae tilted his head. "Understood. And I..." He hesitated. "Would be willing..." He visibly swallowed. "To see how things go."

Even that much seemed to be difficult for Grae to say. Paige got it. He wanted to be the top dog. Literally. Paige wondered if Grae had ever been topped in his life. She would have to ask him next time they got a moment alone. For now, it was as close as they were going to get.

Give and take.

"Well, anyway, we'll be getting to know each other better as we go. Learn each other's secrets. Our fantasies." Paige leaned closer to Grae to trace the thick, raised scar down his torso. "Learn what makes our hearts tick. Or not tick." She stopped at the bottom of the puckered skin, only a couple inches above his navel. "Hold back nothing," she whispered as she met his gaze.

Grae closed his hand over hers, squeezing it slightly, but not moving it away.

She had searched the Internet and found why he had the scar. But she wanted to—no, *needed*—to hear it from his own lips what ended the professional football career of an extremely good player. An up and coming player, as the media had called him.

Grae gave a slight shake to his head. "Another time."

To say Paige felt disappointed was an understatement. It showed Grae wasn't comfortable enough around them to discuss his past. It was heart surgery. Why so close-mouthed?

"Okay, then." She moved back up and leaned farther to trace the raised branding on his right bicep. The chest scar might have been necessary and unplanned, but in contrast, the branding seemed to be planned, unnecessary torture. Not that she didn't like tattoos on men, but being branded was a whole different level. "What about this?"

"It's a branding," was his dry answer.

Connor snorted. Without looking, Paige smacked him in the arm, which made him laugh even harder.

Paige pinched Grae lightly next to the raised skin. "Very funny. I know it's a branding. How about the what, why, when, and whatever were you thinking?"

Grae snagged her fingers and lifted them to his lips. He kissed each tip then sucked her index finger into his mouth.

Paige almost moaned as his tongue swirled sensuously around

her digit. She tamped down her desire to jump onto his lap and finish what he just started. Her voice sounded raspy to her own ears when she said, "You're just trying to avoid the questions."

He smiled around her finger before releasing it. "Not at all."

Paige made a tsking sound, not believing him.

"Fine." He linked his hand with hers, placing them on his thickly muscled thigh.

As she stared at their entwined hands, she reached out with her left to find Connor's, connecting the three of them.

"I will answer your questions. But you must answer one of mine first. And I want you to answer it honestly. Hold nothing back."

Oh, like he did with his surgery scar?

"Shoot," she said.

"What is your deepest, darkest fantasy? Forbidden or not."

Now she quickly regretted it after she heard the question. "Wanting a threesome isn't enough?"

"No."

She peeked toward her husband, who had straightened a little as if he couldn't wait to hear the answer. She might have to turn it around and ask them the same question. Suddenly, she did feel very curious how they would answer. A thrill went through her.

This could get interesting. "Can I have time to think about it?"

Grae blinked at her. "You need time to figure out your ultimate fantasy?"

Sort of. The reason she wanted time was she had a feeling whatever she told him would end up coming true. And this scared her a little, but she wasn't telling him that. "Please. But..." She gave him a serious look. "I don't want to be the only one of us revealing secrets. I want to hear both of yours also. No matter what it is."

Grae's eyes narrowed and darkened for a moment. "I can agree with that as long as none of us judges the other for the answer. Connor?"

"Sure. I'm game."

Paige knew this wasn't a game at all. Definitely some serious shit from way down deep in Grae and once again, a tinge of apprehension crept up her spine. "Okay. The branding?" she prodded him, attempting to steer the conversation back.

"You swear not to avoid my question?"

"Yes. I promise I will reveal my deepest, darkest fantasy." If Paige had a free hand, she would've crossed her fingers and drew an X over her heart.

"The what and when... The brand represents my college fraternity, Omega Psi Phi. If you look closely, you'll see quite a few black football players with brands. The why is simple... It gives us solidarity. Brothers for life."

"I see it now." The Greek letter that stood for Omega was what had been burned into his flesh. "Do you still keep in touch with everyone?"

"Only a few. It's an international fraternity, there are hundreds of chapters."

"That had to be very painful," Connor said.

"It wasn't pleasant," Grae agreed, mildly.

He was downplaying it. Paige knew it had to hurt like a bitch. Who in their right mind gave themselves a third degree burn? "Would you do it again?"

"It doesn't matter. It's done."

Sigh. He certainly didn't give up information easily. He didn't want to admit any regrets he may have? By now, she knew he had no other marks on his body, besides the surgery scar and the one piercing in his ear. Paige realized it was rare to come across a pro football player without any tattoos.

Yes, this man was unique in many ways. She couldn't wait to peel away his many layers to find the true Graedon Ward.

CHAPTER 6

As Grae slid the key into the lock and turned it, he wondered how this happened. It wasn't supposed to end up this way.

He stepped over the threshold into his new *temporary* home. His intent had been for them to move in with him. Instead, he ended up here in middle-class suburbia.

He walked into the kitchen and threw his keys on the counter.

He loved his house, especially his master bedroom suite. It was all warm tones, wood, and rich colors. Expensive furniture and pieces of art.

This house, in contrast, was light and airy, full of windows, floral tones and just…not him.

Luckily, it was only temporary, he thought, as he pulled the refrigerator door open to stare absently into its cool interior. He needed a drink after the cluster of a day he had at work, but all his good liquor was at home. Instead, he was assaulted by a bunch of beer bottles from local breweries, all lined up like good little soldiers.

Grae tamped down his disappointment. His options were to hit the local liquor store or drive the forty-five minutes home to get the good stuff. Or find a local joint that served top shelf gin or scotch.

He gazed down at his watch. It would be at least an hour before Paige would arrive home. Longer for Connor. Especially since the man flew to St. Louis this morning for his job.

This meant Paige and he would have the house to themselves for the next few days. His spirits mysteriously brightened.

Maybe he should head out to the farm and surprise her. Take her to dinner. Wine and dine her before ravishing her for the rest of the night. He pictured her with her hair loose and messy, her eyelids hooded, her mouth parted, crying out for him as he pounded her hard and fast, her nails raking his skin, her teeth tearing at his flesh.

Grae dropped a hand to the bulge in his pants. His cock was stirring and he no longer needed a drink. He needed Paige.

He snagged his keys from the counter and drove his X6 like a madman to the farm.

When he arrived, he found the building that held the business offices empty and locked. Ty and Logan's house wasn't far, just down a gravel driveway, so he figured he could drive by there and check if Paige's car was out front. When he pulled up to the sprawling log home, her red SUV was there, as well as a few others.

In fact, when he approached the front door, it sounded like a party was going on. Grae's temper flared a bit at the thought of Paige being at a party that he knew nothing about. He closed his eyes, took a calming breath, and let himself in the door of his friend's house.

Loud voices and what sounded like a televised football game came from the living room and he headed that direction. He realized no one heard him come in, nor knew he stood behind them in the entrance to the great room.

His anger bubbled up again as he realized Paige was the only woman in the room. Yes, this was her brother's house. And yes, she was in this house often. He recognized this fact. But Paige was sitting on the couched curled up against Ty White. Sandwiched on the other side was Ren Landis, another retired NFL player. Perched at the end of the couch was Cole Dixon, Ren's lover and also a former Boston Bulldog. Quinn, Eve, nor her brother Logan, were anywhere to be found.

His hands shook and he curled his fingers into fists to hide it as he moved to stand behind the couch, staring down at the arm Ty had around Paige.

Ty must have sensed him standing there because he twisted his head in surprise. Then he smiled and greeted him. "Hey, brother."

Paige looked over her shoulder at him and said his name, her brows furrowed.

Grae pinned Ty with a stare. "Don't *hey, brother* me when you are on the couch with an arm around my woman."

"Your woman?" Ren echoed, looking at Ty in surprise. "I thought she was married to Connor. Did I miss something?"

Paige frowned at Grae. "Hey, he's like my brother. In fact, he's my *brother*-in-law. What's wrong with you?"

Movement on the TV made him glance up. The game playing was all too familiar to him. He stepped around the couch to grab Paige to remove her from the house—but he was too late.

His lips flattened as he watched Paige's expression change from annoyed to horrified, as she watched Grae collapse on the field.

Grae didn't need to turn around to know everything that happened next. At least what he could remember. The rest he himself had watched over and over on tape, trying to figure out what happened on the day that ended his promising career.

The sports announcer's words echoed the scene he relived in his head.

The refs called a medical time-out. The team's medical staff rushed out to surround him, quickly followed by a stretcher. He laid on the ground encircled by bodies of concerned medical staff, coaches, and teammates. Someone rushed up with an AED and tried to shock his heart back to beating. Two other people took turns doing CPR between the body-jolting shocks.

Paige watched in horror as the scene before her unfolded, a shaky hand covering her mouth, her eyes wide.

People on the screen were yelling, waving their arms, and a cart was rushed out to take Grae away. The filled stadium was in complete silence. Both teams were on their knees in prayer circles. One teammate had collapsed to the ground, pounding on the turf. Paige couldn't make out what he yelled but he screamed up at the sky. She turned in slow motion to Ty.

He was that player.

Her brother-in-law squeezed her shoulders in support.

Paige brushed away the wetness on her cheeks; she hadn't even realized she was crying. She willed Grae to fight to live, even though he stood feet from her, perfectly fine. Her chest tightened as her fingers dug into Ty's arm. She wanted to turn away but she couldn't.

She couldn't.

When Grae was finally carted off the field and off screen, Paige turned teary eyes to the man who stood stiffly near the couch, his hands clenched into fists, his expression blank.

She reached out for him.

He stepped back. "I'll meet you at home." He spun on his heels and strode from the room.

"Grae!" she called out, but he ignored her.

As she heard the front door slam, she jumped to her feet to follow him. To stop him from leaving. To apologize.

Ty snagged her arm and she fell back onto the couch. He wrapped her into his arms, whispering, "Let him go, baby girl. Just let him cool down for a bit."

Ren leaned forward to look her in the face and asked, "Damn, Paige, he didn't tell you?"

Paige shook her head. "No, I asked, he didn't want to talk about it. I did some Google searches and knew the basics, but I never saw the actual film."

"If I would have known, I wouldn't have brought the damn tape over," Ren said, shaking his head. "Or I would have given you a copy to watch with him. I didn't know it was going to cause a problem."

"I didn't either," Paige murmured against Ty's chest.

"I don't get it, " Cole said, squatting at Paige's feet, his hands squeezing her knees. "What is he to you?"

"Our lover."

G rae sat on the couch in the dark. If it wasn't for the movement of him raising a glass to his lips, she might not have spotted him.

She stopped at the entrance of the room, waiting. Waiting… For him to say something, to invite her in. Anything.

As the seconds ticked by, her first instinct was to apologize. But honestly, there was nothing for her to be sorry about. She did nothing wrong.

It was only natural to want to know everything about her lover. Yes, maybe she should have waited until he was ready to tell her. Or maybe she should've waited until Connor was home. But she didn't.

Also, knowing that Ren and Ty had played ball with him, she couldn't resist asking.

She chewed on her bottom lip.

"Don't."

The sharp command caused her to release her lip. She rubbed

her hands in frustration over her face. She would not apologize. She. Would. Not.

"Why? Why did you go to them?" His voice sounded deep and low, wounded. She'd broken his trust.

Yes, trust was needed one hundred percent in a polyamorous relationship. When Logan and Ty found out that Grae was moving in with them—*temporarily*—they had emphasized the trust issue to her. And not just once either.

She didn't wait for an invite, she decided enough was enough and she entered the room to stand in front of him. As her eyes adjusted to the dark, she realized he had his elbows on his thighs and his drink hanging loosely from his fingers between his knees.

His gaze was directed downward toward the floor. After a heartbeat, he lifted his head, emptied the glass, and put it aside on the table next to the couch. "I would have told you." He pounded on his chest with the flat of his palm. "Me," he emphasized, his voice raised slightly. "There was no reason for you to find out from them."

"But it wasn't a secret. It happened on national TV."

"You didn't even give me a chance."

"How long was I supposed to wait, Grae? How long? Medical issues happen every day."

"But not to me."

His words ripped her apart. She could feel his pain and defeat. The frustration of losing a career because of a fault he had no control over. She dropped to her knees in front him. "Why? Because you were in shape? You were an athlete? Did you think you were immune?"

"It destroyed my career."

"What could you have done differently?"

He shook his head and averted his gaze from her.

Paige closed her eyes, taking a couple breaths before looking at him again.

His body looked stiff and he had shut down.

"*Jesus*, Grae. There was nothing you could've done about it."

Her words were met with silence.

She placed her hands on his knees and leaned closer. "From what I've read, you had an undetected congenital heart defect. You couldn't have known. No one knew. Not even the doctors you went to since you were an infant. Your heart failure would have happened at some point, whether you were on the field or not. But you lived, Grae, *you lived*. And you know why? Because you were in that game, on that field, when you collapsed. You were surrounded by medical personnel. Not alone in your car or at your home. Otherwise, you wouldn't be here right now." She swallowed hard. "You wouldn't be here with me...with us."

Grae shot to his feet, almost knocking Paige on her ass, but before she could stand, he grabbed her, threw her over his shoulder, and rushed down the hallway. He kicked the master bedroom door wide and threw her on the bed.

Her breath caught and adrenaline pumped through her body. She scrambled backward while he tore off his clothes. She reached for the light sweater she wore but his sudden, sharp, "No," stopped her.

Once naked, he pounced onto the bed and crawled until he reached her. He yanked her sweater over her head and threw it. He ripped off her bra, breaking the clasp, and tossed that somewhere too.

She only helped by lifting her hips enough so he could peel her jeans down her legs, after removing her shoes and socks. One shoe landed on the dresser, knocking over some of Connor's cologne. She swore he growled as she watched him move up and over her—so solidly built, the muscles bunching underneath his dark skin, the overhead light making his body gleam as he shifted.

His body was so fucking amazing and she was so fucking wet for him. As long as he didn't hurt her, she didn't care how rough he got. She liked it.

Fuck, she loved it.

He was the complete opposite of Connor and Grae's dominance thrilled her. Made her want him more than ever. No matter what she was in the mood for she got it. Tenderness from Connor. Power and authority from Grae.

Grae slid his hands over her shoulders, down her arms, until he got to her wrists. He circled them with his fingers and pulled her arms over her head. He pinned her wrists down to the mattress with one hand, while his other grabbed a fistful of hair, pulling her head back, forcing her neck to arch.

His gaze was intense as he stared down at her, not saying a word, not making a sound.

Her lips parted, her breath rushing in and out from between them.

"What do you want from me?" His question sounded raw, almost painful.

It sent a shudder through her. "You," she breathed. "I want all of you."

He dipped his head and sank his teeth into her neck at the same time driving his cock deep inside her.

She was wet, but she wasn't ready. She gasped as he filled her, stretching her, thrusting hard and fast. She struggled to free her arms, wanting to hold on to him, but he held them tighter.

Grae sucked her skin where he'd bitten her, then lifted his head to watch her while his body entered her over and over. He pounded her relentlessly. "I'm giving you all of me. This is what you wanted."

"Yes," she hissed, her teeth grabbing her bottom lip.

He crushed his lips against hers, taking her mouth, licking her lip.

A groan built at the back of her throat.

He suddenly released her wrists and she grabbed his ass, her fingers digging hard into the muscles that flexed with each thrust.

Before she could wrap her legs around his thighs, he rolled them both over, bringing her on top. They stilled, and she looked down at him. His hands were on her hips, holding her against him. In this position, he felt unbearably deep. The pleasure just on the edge of painful. She ground her pelvis in a circle, and cupped her breasts, pushing the mounds together. She pinched both nipples between her thumbs and forefingers and twisted them, pulled them as he watched her, his eyes hooded but very aware.

His cock twitched inside her as if she needed a reminder of her role. She braced her hands on his chest and…

The scar was thick and raised, the shiny skin a shade of eggplant. Paige shivered envisioning Graedon's chest being cracked open and spread apart wide. His sick heart beating in the doctor's hands before he died. He *did* die a small death before a stranger's heart could be placed in his body, bringing him back to life once again.

Like she reminded him, he *was* alive. And she could feel just how alive beneath her. His heart beat strong under her palm; his erection like steel, filled with the lifeblood that his borrowed heart pumped through his veins.

She circled her hips once more, her inner walls clenching down, tightening around him. Then she rose and lowered, tilting her hips, directing him to where she wanted him. An ache built within her as she rode him hard, his cock hitting her most sensitive spot. Not only was she slick with sweat, but also her own arousal as she drove herself down on him.

His fingers gripped her flesh, his arms flexed with each rise and fall. His stomach muscles tensed and released. And he watched her, his heated gaze never wavering. "I want to watch you come apart."

Between the deep rumble of his voice and his words, she shattered into a million pieces. She ground against him harder as she rode out the waves of her orgasm, driving him deeper.

He sat up, wrapped an arm around her waist, and twisted her onto her belly underneath him. He pulled her hips back and towards him, running a finger between her swollen folds. "You are so wet. I want to taste you."

She pushed her face into the mattress as his tongue stroked her sensitive flesh, his thumb pressed against her clit, circling, flicking. Her cry was muffled in the sheets, her hands fisting the fabric tight when his tongue entered her, tasted her. He sucked at the plump folds, and as he pinched her clit once more, a climax spiraled through her, making her toes curl, curving her spine.

"That's it, baby. Give it all to me. Let me taste your pleasure." With a last stroke of his tongue, he shifted behind her, reaching for something.

She heard the nightstand drawer slide open and the cap of the Astroglide they kept stored there snap open. She turned her head enough to see what he was doing. He had the long, black vibrating anal plug in his hand and he was liberally coating it with lube. He moved back behind her and with a lubed finger, he pressed against her anus, preparing her.

Paige's nipples hardened even more at the thought of what was about to happen. She'd been anxious to try the new toy, even though it had been actually purchased to help prepare Connor.

The plug hummed when he turned it on. He rubbed it over her tight opening and she moaned at the unfamiliar sensation. Then there was pressure as he slowly worked the long, thin toy inside her. She could feel the vibrations to her core, and she wanted nothing more than Grae to be inside her at the same time. "Fuck me," she demanded.

Grae ignored her and worked the plug in and out of her, dribbling more lube on the toy, it's coolness against her heated skin even more of a turn-on.

He pulled the plug almost completely out and Paige screamed into the bed in frustration.

Then she grunted when he thrust his cock into her and pushed the toy to its hilt at the same time. She came instantly, her body clenching around him, around the vibrator.

He stilled, waiting for her body to relax again, and then he held the toy deep inside her while he pounded her from behind, his other hand holding her hip in place to take his onslaught. His fingers would leave a bruise, but she didn't care.

The vibrations deep inside her drove her wild, drove her to the edge again and again.

Until she couldn't take anymore.

Her body was spent and Grae had slowed. She felt a bead of his sweat drip onto her ass and heard his labored breathing. His endurance amazed her.

He made a sound, then ground out, "I'm going to come deep inside you." With one last thrust, he stilled, his fingers flexing along her hip, his cock pulsing inside her. "You're mine, Paige."

And that's when it hit her.

He hadn't worn a condom.

CHAPTER 7

Paige could hear the smile in Connor's voice as they had their nightly phone call. Whenever Connor was out of town, they made a point to talk to each other every day. Even if the conversation was just about boring work stuff. Paige simply needed to hear his voice no matter what he was talking about.

"Have you and Grae been having a lot of sex when I've been gone?"

Oh, man, what a loaded question. Do you admit to your husband you've been having copious amounts of sex with another man in his absence? But it was the agreement and Paige wanted to always be upfront with him.

She shot a look at Grae, who laid relaxed on the couch, watching some game film on the large flat screen. The coffee table had a pile of files and loose papers, and on top of the paper mountain was an iPad. He had the TV muted. Paige wondered if it was to be courteous because of Connor's phone call, or if he just wanted to listen in.

"Yes," she answered.

A smile spread wide across Grae's face, even though his gaze hadn't moved from the TV screen.

"I miss you two."

"We miss you also, Connor. We can't wait for you to come home." Paige assumed Grae felt the same way as she did. And if he didn't, too bad. No reason for Connor to know that.

"Maybe I can Skype in and participate from afar. You know I like watching the two of you together."

Paige turned her back to Grae, whispering, "That sounds like an exciting plan, honey. We'd have to set things up with the computer and all."

"So do it and text me when you're ready."

Paige sighed. Nothing like having scheduled sex. "Okay, I'll let you know."

They finished the call and hung up. Then she faced Grae.

He had paused the DVD and watched her instead. "Let him know what?" he asked.

"He wants us to set up the computer to Skype in."

"Okay."

"And he wants to watch us having sex."

Grae raised his chin. "Ah." He sat up. "Don't whisper when you're on the phone with him. There can't be any secrets between us."

Paige only nodded and slapped her phone against her thigh. She started to pace the length of the room. "What about the condom issue?"

Grae pinned his eyebrows together. "What issue?"

"About you not using one."

"Not an issue. Connor doesn't wear one when he's with you."

Paige snagged her bottom lip with her teeth.

"Paige." Her name became a warning.

She sighed and released her lip. "Grae..."

"*Paige*," he dragged out her name.

"We need to tell him."

"It shouldn't matter," he said.

"I realize it was something we didn't discuss..."

"Does it bother you?" he asked.

She thought about it for a moment. Did it bother her? No, in the end it didn't. At first, she'd felt uncertain, but after the last couple days of condom-less sex, she didn't even give a thought. However, she was more concerned about Connor's reaction. "No." She hesitated. "But anal—"

"That's different. A condom will always be used."

She moved over to the couch and climbed onto his lap.

Grae wrapped his arms around her hips and placed a kiss on her shoulder. "We can use a condom tonight, but be aware why it's going to be used." He gave her a sly smile.

Paige smacked his chest. "Yeah, I get what you're saying there, big boy. If I make you wear a condom, you'll be doing a little backdoor action."

"Little?" he chuckled.

She made a sound and she pressed her face into the crook of his neck, inhaling his scent. "And that's a good reason why not to wear a condom tonight."

"Thought so. But don't think you're going to get a reprieve forever."

Grae's cock felt as hard as steel under her ass. The thought of him taking her from behind must be getting him in the mood. Not that he was never in the mood. This man was always ready for action. Ever since he *temporarily* moved into the house a week ago, there hadn't been one night where everyone just got under the covers and went to sleep. Now, with Connor gone, not one morning either. She went to work with her ass dragging and an oversized cup of java.

Ty and Logan had laughed at her, reminding her how much *work* was involved in a threesome. Work being code for sex, of course. But it wasn't so much Connor who was demanding. It was Grae. He expected it every night—and it was never a quickie.

Look at her complaining... How many women would want to

be in her shoes, getting the attention of two intelligent, sexy men? Getting spoiled and having multiple orgasms every night.

Any woman who wasn't bat shit crazy.

She traced his goatee. Even though she didn't like facial hair, she had to admit there were some perks to his when his face was buried between her thighs. Her pussy clenched at the thought. She squirmed in his lap, causing him to tighten his grip on her hips. She turned to straddle him on the couch, so she could look at him directly.

His easy smile was a little bit of a relief for her. She knew he hadn't been thrilled about moving into their house *temporarily*, instead of the other way around. But it had just seemed easier at the time.

Though Paige figured if things worked out well between the three of them, she and Connor would move into his house eventually since it was much larger. Plus, the fact Grae continually emphasized his moving in was only temporary.

His master bedroom was no doubt larger than theirs. With the sheer size of his place, there would be plenty of room for the three of them and their belongings. In contrast with their house, where Grae's clothes and personal items were in a spare bedroom closet and in the hallway bathroom.

The positives of him living with them would be him being within fingertip range when it came to physical contact. The downside was that Paige was hardly ever alone anymore. She sometimes enjoyed having the house to herself when Connor was out of town.

Okay, maybe more than sometimes. It was nice to sit on the couch, watching sappy chick flicks, eating a whole pint of Ben & Jerry's ice cream with a box of tissues next to her. Something she would never do with Connor or Grae at home. Plus, Grae always kept track of where she was. Whether they were at the house or not. She didn't think it was a trust issue, but more of a possessiveness issue. This man was all about control.

In one way, it was exciting. In another, it sometimes felt stifling. Connor wasn't like that and she wasn't used to it. She hoped it was just the newness of the relationship and he would loosen up as time went on.

"You're wearing a frown," he said, running a thumb over her bottom lip.

She hadn't even been aware of it. She shook her head. "It's nothing."

"Paige." Again, with the warning tone.

"Grae, leave it alone. Okay?"

He regarded her for a moment before saying, "Okay."

Paige practically sighed with relief. "Thanks."

He placed a finger under her chin and lifted it until she met his eyes again. "You know you can always talk to me, tell me what's bothering you, right?"

"Yes."

"And will you?"

"Sure."

"Promise?" he asked as if he didn't believe her.

"I promise."

He smiled at her. "Good. That's all I can ask for."

"Grae, you can tell us stuff also, you know."

"I understand."

No, she didn't want to hear that he understood the concept of a two-way street; she wanted him to promise the same thing as she did. She got a feeling he held back things, personal things like his heart failure. Paige placed a hand over the left side of his chest. "Do you know whose heart is beating in your body?"

He placed a hand over hers and squeezed her fingers. "I do."

His answer caused goosebumps to break out all over her body. She wondered what it was like to have a piece of someone else living within you. The concept was disturbing, but fascinating as well. "Tell me." She placed an ear against his chest. She wanted to hear his heartbeat as he told her the story, as well as feel the vibrations of his deep, low voice.

"His name was Brandon. He was only twenty-two years old and a junior in college."

"What was his major?"

"Education. He was studying to be a high school teacher. I was told he was extremely smart. Aced his SATs. Tutored on the side to make some cash. He could speak Spanish and Italian fluently. He was a Humanist at heart. Always looking to help the less fortunate. He would run blanket and coat drives in winter, food drives in summer. Things like that. He would go without if someone needed it more than him. His mother told me that one Christmas, he took all of his gifts, clothes, toys, whatever he got, and donated it all to a shelter."

"So he was a Saint."

"Pretty much."

"So, what happened?" she asked, though she feared his answer. She already knew Brandon's story didn't end well, but Grae's did.

"He was driving home from school for Thanksgiving break and a drunk driver hit him. Blew right through a red light, T-boned Brandon's car on the driver's side, doing about sixty miles-per-hour. Brandon never had a chance to avoid the accident."

"He didn't suffer," Paige said, hoping it was true.

"No."

"Were his other organs also given to people in need?"

"Yes. He lives through a bunch of different people now. His life was his ultimate donation. He helped quite a few needy people, probably in ways he never would have expected. At least at that age. He was way too young." Grae stopped talking and his chest rose and fell with his steady breath.

Paige absorbed everything he just told her. "I would love to thank his family."

"I will bring you along next time I visit."

She lifted her head to look up at him. "Really? You actually visit his family?"

He shrugged, then tucked a section of her hair behind her ear. "They asked me to. Sometimes his mother presses her ear against my chest and listens to her son's heart beating. It's a piece of him still alive, though inside of me."

"I guess that helped them to cope. To know that their son was still helping others, even after death."

"I started a charity to help the homeless in his name," he said quietly.

Paige pushed up to a seated position. "Really? Why haven't you mentioned it?"

"There hasn't been a reason to bring it up until now. I have people managing it and Brandon's family and extended family are very involved. They practically run it. I basically help fund it."

"Fucking Grae, that's just crazy good. You're an awesome man."

"No." He kissed her forehead. "Just a man."

"Oh, whatever," she scoffed. It amazed her how he could be so tender with her outside of the bedroom. But inside the bedroom…a whole different story.

Then this thought brought her back to Connor wanting to Skype when she and Grae were having sex tonight and wondering if she should give him the heads up about the condom thing. "Well, we can test that ticker of yours tonight."

He chuckled. "Yes, we will."

Her grin turned back into a frown.

He shook his head. "Seriously Paige. Stop worrying about Connor and the condom *issue*. He's a reasonable man."

That he was. But still…

She sighed and wrapped her arms around his neck, grinding her pelvis against his crotch. "Should we do a quickie on the couch before the big show?"

His eyelids shuttered as he studied her. "We could. But once we start, I'm not sure how much of a quickie it's going to be. Once I'm deep inside you, I don't want to rush. And I don't think your couch is waterproof."

Waterproof? Huh?

Oooh. Yes. Her responsiveness to his touch, his actions.

She circled her hips over his lap again. "You mean how wet I get when you're playing with me, eating me, fucking me?"

He lifted his chin slightly, his fingers tightening up on her hips. He thrust up against her, so she could feel how hard he was. "You're being slightly conservative with the term 'wet.'"

Paige laughed. "You think?"

"I know."

"Are you going to throw me over your shoulder again and take me to bed, big boy?"

His lips split into a wide smile, his beautiful white teeth contrasting against his broad, dark cherry lips. Lips that tasted as good as they looked. In fact, she needed to sample them right this minute. She pressed her hands on his chest and leaned into him, brushing her breasts against him as she slid her tongue along his very skilled mouth.

His smile quickly disappeared when he brought a hand to the back of her head, and claimed her mouth as his. He controlled the kiss completely. The pressure, the deepness, the tangling of their tongues. His fingers dug into her hair, tugging her head back so he could rake his teeth along her jawline and down her throat. He murmured something against her skin, but she had no idea what it was. Right now, she remained too focused on his mouth, as he nipped where her shoulder met her neck. A shiver overcame her, making her nipples pebble painfully.

His erection felt hard and thick beneath her—and there were too many layers of clothing separating them. She whimpered in frustration, pulling at his shirt, letting him know that she wanted him. She wanted him now.

He stood up and she gripped her arms tighter around his neck, wrapping her legs around his waist as he moved down the hallway towards the bedroom. When he got to the bed, he placed her on the mattress and moved away.

"Get undressed."

"But Connor—"

"Now."

As she pulled off her clothing, then watched as he moved to the nightstand to yank open the drawer. He pulled out her purple vibrator—her favorite one—and tossed it onto the bed beside her.

Her heart and her breath sped up as she finished pulling off her clothes. "I need to text Connor…Skype…"

"You need to do what I tell you."

Blood rushed into Paige's head, making her slightly dizzy. Her pussy clenched and a rush of wetness was felt at her core. This man's demanding words could turn her into a puddle of arousal.

She brushed both of her nipples with her palms and spread her legs to show him how wet he made her.

He stood at the end of the bed, watching her, his expression closed. "You're going to do everything I tell you."

"Yes."

"Everything Connor tells you."

"Yes," she hissed.

"I want you to make yourself come using your vibrator while I set up the laptop and text Connor."

Paige closed her eyes and nodded. She wanted to squeeze her thighs together to rid herself of some of the building ache. But she also wanted to keep herself splayed open, so he can see everything, all of her.

She reached for her vibrator. The one that twisted while it vibrated and had the extra special addition on it to stimulate her clit. She could climax in seconds when using this one. She never used it on herself in front of Grae or Connor. She'd only used it when she'd been alone.

She brushed it along her damp folds, letting the toy get slick, so it would penetrate her easily. The anticipation of knowing an orgasm was just seconds away made her toes curl and her body tremor. She pressed the buttons to turn on the vibration and slid the head of the toy to her entrance. Before she could slide it deep inside, Grae ripped his shirt over his head, tossed it on the dresser, and walked out.

The bulge in his jeans had been unmistakable. Paige smiled. Just as she slipped the purple vibrator inside her, he returned, laptop in his hands. She then pushed the buttons to make the toy twist.

He ignored her as he set the computer up on the dresser and made sure the camera captured the bed and what Paige was doing clearly.

Her hips lifted off of the mattress as the intense vibrations stimulated both inside and her clit at once. She let out a small cry as the combination of circling movement and the pulses of the toy brought her to the edge quickly.

His back was to her, but he said, "Don't you dare come without telling me."

She bit her bottom lip and let out a curse. "I'm coming, Grae. *Fuck*, I'm coming. Watch me."

When he turned, the toy, as well as the thought of him and Connor watching, caused her whole body to explode.

She was a naughty exhibitionist, giving them a show. The image made her inner walls ripple even more intensely. She pulled out the vibrator, turned it off, and threw it to the other side of the bed. Her clit was too sensitive now to use it. She was ready for the real thing anyway.

"Connor, can you see your wife?" Grae asked.

Paige raised her gaze to the laptop screen.

Her husband was in some motel room, somewhere on the west coast, watching his wife about to get fucked by another man. "Yes. You're beautiful when you come, baby," he said. His Adam's apple bounced as he swallowed hard.

"She's already warmed up. Are you ready to watch me fuck her, Connor?" As Grae spoke, he removed the rest of his clothes until he stood at the edge of the bed completely naked, his erection thick and hard, pointing in Paige's direction.

Connor didn't answer him.

Grae turned his head slightly towards the camera. "Connor, what do you want your wife to do?"

"Anything. Everything."

"Be more specific," Grae demanded.

"I want… I want her to take you into her mouth. And then I want to watch you spank her until her ass is red and then fuck her so hard until she can't take anymore… Goddamn, I wish I was there."

"Just imagine if you were here, Connor, you could be spanking her ass and fucking her while she's sucking me."

A rush went through her at Grae's words. When Connor said nothing, she glanced at the laptop. Connor's eyes were closed and it looked as though he was fumbling with something off screen. Paige had no doubt what he was doing. She knew how turned on he became while watching her and Grae.

"Come here," Grae said to her.

She scrambled to the end of the bed and sat on the edge.

Grae stepped closer, between her thighs, his cock a hair's breadth from her lips. "You heard your husband."

Paige circled the base of his erection with her fingers and squeezed as she licked the plump crown. She took him into her mouth and his hands buried in her hair. She tried to breathe calmly through her nose as he forced her head up and down his length.

She lifted her gaze as she worked him with her tongue and lips, sucking him hard and then lightly, varying her technique.

His dark eyes were hooded, his mouth a tight slash, a muscle in his jaw ticked. His fingers tightened against her scalp. "Is this what you wanted, Connor?" Grae asked, without looking towards the screen.

"Yes," came Connor's groan.

"You wanted to see me fuck your wife's face?"

A strangled sound came from the laptop, but Paige didn't bother to look. She couldn't. Grae was now controlling the pace of her sucking. He controlled how deep she took him. He hit the back of her throat over and over as he pulled her head to meet his thrusting hips.

Paige struggled to relax her throat in an attempt to keep from gagging. But it was pointless. Paige slapped his thigh. She was tapping out.

Grae's thrusts shallowed and he asked gruffly, "Have you had enough?" He stepped back to let her answer.

Except she didn't, she only nodded as she caught her breath.

"Was that enough for you, Connor?"

Paige glanced at the computer again.

Connor's face looked flushed and he nodded slowly.

Grae asked Connor, "Have you come yet?"

"Almost… No. Soon."

"We'll take care of that shortly. I promise. What do you want me to use to spank her? Belt, hand, paddle?"

We have a paddle?

And no fucking way on the belt.

"Just your hand," Connor said.

Paige sighed in relief. Erotic spanking had always turned her on. But being turned on and being "punished" were two different things.

"Get on the bed, Paige. On your hands and knees."

She hesitated and regarded his serious expression. Thoughts spun through her mind.

"Paige, get on the bed," he commanded slowly, emphasizing each word. "I won't hurt you."

She closed her eyes for a split second. Of course, he wouldn't hurt her. She trusted him in that way. He wanted their sex play to be exciting, not a turn-off. As controlling and dominant as Grae was, he had never gone over the top with her. Or with Connor. There was a line he never crossed.

Grae pointed to the bed and Paige crawled to the center, facing the headboard on her hands and knees. Her body started to shake in anticipation of what was to come.

The bed sank behind her under his weight. She could feel the heat radiating off him. His body burned like a furnace next to her skin.

Being naked on all fours left her completely exposed to him. It took forever for him to touch her.

When he did, it was to drag a finger between her folds to check how wet she was. "Connor, you should feel how much she wants this. Don't you, Paige?"

"Yes," she said with a moan.

He spanked her pussy lightly and the surprise of the unexpected made her gasp. It also made her beg for more. His fingers slapping her sensitive mound was something she'd never experienced, but it shot lightning through her with each hard tap. "Oh my God," Paige cried out.

"You like that." It wasn't a question.

Sometimes she thought he knew her body better than she did. This was not the spanking she'd expected. "Yes. I love it."

His fingers disappeared and without warning his tongue stroked her stinging flesh, teasing her clit for a moment. Then this was quickly replaced by his hand again, and a harder slap this time.

She jerked forward, gasping. She pushed back to her original position and he did it again and again until her pussy became so stimulated and slick with arousal, she was about to beg him to fuck her.

Then before she could say anything, his palm cracked down on her ass cheek. She cried out at the sting and her inner muscles clenched with the need for him to fill her.

She swallowed hard as he slapped her other cheek.

Grae murmured, "That's it, Paige, look how your skin is turning pink." He raised his voice a little. "Can you see it, Connor? Can you see how red your wife's ass is?"

Connor called out, "Yes. Yes. More. Do it some more."

Grae covered her body with his, bringing his lips to her ear. "Do you want more, Paige?"

She nodded her head, his words and breath against her ear causing goosebumps to break out along her body.

Yes, I want more, she thought. For a moment, she wondered if there was something wrong with her for wanting this so much. Only it felt like more of a deep sting along her skin, and not pain. An adrenaline rush came with each strike of his palm.

The sound of his hand against her skin was sharp, followed by her low moan. The air in the room cooled her heated skin.

Grae smoothed his hand over both cheeks, then kissed each buttock, his tongue swirling over the area where he'd struck her. "Look how beautiful her ass is like that, Connor."

Paige snuck a peek at the laptop. Connor's face appeared lax and flushed, his arm moving at a rapid pace, though she couldn't see lower than his chest.

"Are you going to come, Connor?" Grae asked him.

"Yes."

"I want you to wait until we all come together."

"I can't..."

"You can," Grae told him, firmly.

Instead of receiving a slap, Grae thrust hard into her, seating himself deep. He grabbed her hips and held them in place as he pounded her hard for a few strokes and then he stilled. He leaned over to trace his tongue down her spine and he kissed the dimples above her ass. "You fit me perfectly, Paige." He leaned over and whispered in her ear again, "You were made for me."

He straightened up and separated her ass cheeks. He pumped into her slowly, taking his time, his hips flexing with each movement. He pressed a thumb against her anus, teasing the tight hole. He reached around with his other hand to thumb her clit at the same time.

The pressure from the front, the pressure from the back, and the fullness inside her, all at the same time made her grip the sheets. She closed her eyes as she was pushed to the point of climax. Her body wanting, needing the release, but not wanting to end these sensations so soon.

"I can feel you tightening around me. Are you about to come?"

"Yes. Yes. I want to come. But I don't want to come either. I can't get enough of what you're doing."

He circled her clit more intensely, then pressed harder against her anus until he pushed past the rim, entering her, his hips pounding a pattern against her ass. "We need to all come together." This time, he didn't sound so collected. The strain in his voice was evident. "Tell me when you're ready."

Paige grunted in frustration. She was oh-so-ready. She just needed to let herself go. Allow herself to fall off that edge she stood on.

"Connor," Grae panted. "Are you ready?"

"Yes," was his ragged answer.

"Paige?"

"Yes. Oh, yes!"

"Connor, I'm going to come deep in your wife...Now!"

The intense pulsations of her orgasm made her cry out. Grae stiffened and grunted behind her as he released deep within her.

Then from what sounded like from a distance, they heard Connor let out a sharp curse.

As Grae pulled out, she collapsed on the bed and turned her head toward the laptop. She took a few deep breaths before calling out to Connor, "I love you, baby."

"I love you too," he answered, sounding exhausted. "But don't think I missed that he didn't use a condom."

Then he shut down Skype.

"I told you," Paige muttered into the sheet.

"I'll handle it," Grae said before Paige heard the soft click of the bathroom door as he closed it.

CHAPTER 8

Connor stared at his wife through wide eyes. He'd met her at the front door when she came home from work. He had arrived home from his west coast trip not even an hour earlier.

After kissing the hell out of her, he fought the urge to drag her through the house back to the bedroom to show her just how much he missed her. He'd only been gone for four nights, though, since Grae lived in the house with them, it had seemed longer than normal. Knowing another man had unfettered access to fuck your wife when you were out of town took a little getting used to.

Last night using the webcam had been hot, and it was a good way to stay involved when he was on a business trip. But...and the big *but* here was, Grae hadn't used a condom, and it hadn't been discussed with Connor before it happened.

So, now, he wanted some answers. There would be no better time than the present since Grae wasn't at the house. "From the beginning, it has been discussed how things need to be kept in the open. Why wasn't this discussed with me first?" He wasn't angry about it, but more like disappointed they hadn't conferred with him.

Paige averted her eyes and reached for the glass of wine on the counter. "It just happened, Connor. I'm sorry we didn't say something first."

Not only did she seem sorry, but she also sounded a bit guilty. Maybe this hadn't been her decision either. "What if you get pregnant?" He wasn't quite ready to think about Paige having another man's baby. And he may never be. Logan and Ty had a beautiful child with Quinn, not to mention another on the way, and no one cared who the biological father was. Connor wasn't so sure it would be so easy for them.

But what the hell? The relationship was *way* too new to be thinking about pregnancies and children anyway. Who knew, though, maybe Grae was clipped? A temporary sense of relief overcame him at the possibility.

"I'm on the pill," she reminded him.

"I know. But it's not a hundred percent reliable."

"But neither are condoms."

"But used together—"

"Connor," Paige said, sounding a little impatient with him. She took a long sip of wine, put the glass down, and came to stand in front of him.

"Paige." He didn't want to start an argument. That wasn't what this was about. He wanted what was best for their relationship, whether it included Grae or not. No matter what happened between the three of them, he didn't want anything to destroy their marriage, their relationship, their connection.

He reached out and grabbed her arms, pulling her into his embrace. He leaned back against the kitchen wall, holding her tight. "What if you get pregnant and it's not mine," he murmured.

"I'm not going to get pregnant, honey. I haven't gotten pregnant in all these years. The pill has been reliable for me."

Connor sighed. "You trust him enough to have unprotected sex, Paige? I mean, the three of us are intimate. Are you sure he's not having sex outside of our relationship?"

"First, you scare her with the possibility of getting pregnant, and now you want to spread doubts of my fidelity?" The deep voice and heated words came from the hallway.

Connor's heart stopped. He expected Paige to immediately pull away from him, but she didn't. They both looked over their shoulders to the man in the kitchen entranceway.

"What are you worried about, Connor?" Grae asked, leaning against the doorway, his arms crossed over his chest. He must have come straight from the gym; his shoulders looked beefed up more than ever. "Why would you think that I'd begin a relationship with you and Paige and then turn around and step out? You two should be all I need. And the same goes for you both."

Paige smoothed a hand over Connor's chest before pulling away. "Believe me, the two of you are *plenty* enough for me. Especially since I don't want to end up crippled." She rolled her eyes and chuckled. She snagged her wineglass and took another healthy swallow. She turned to face him. "Connor, Grae and I discussed it yesterday, and I did want to give you the heads up."

Grae pushed off the wall and entered the room, stopping in front of Connor. The freaking man was so much bigger than him. Connor was no wimp, but he wasn't a muscular beast either, and sometimes Grae's presence intimidated him.

Then again, he had to admit it excited him too.

Connor eyeballed the larger man. "You two discussed it but didn't ask me how I felt."

"No, we didn't," Grae admitted. "And that's my fault, not Paige's. I told her I would handle it."

"Interesting choice of words, Grae. Handle it or handle me?"

Grae tilted his head and brushed a hand over his goatee. "Do you want me to sugar coat it?"

They regarded each other and for a moment, neither said a word. It was a testosterone showdown.

Connor wasn't backing down. Not here. Not this time. They had been in the wrong, not him.

Grae shifted his weight forward.

Connor held steady, merely inches from him.

Finally, Grae released a breath and instead of backing away from Connor, stepped closer.

Connor could feel Grae's heat radiate against his skin, even through his clothes.

"I apologize," Grae said after a moment. "This is all my fault. I should have sought and respected your opinion on this matter."

Connor's brows knitted together. What? Did he just win a face-off with Grae? Or was Grae simply trying to keep the peace?

Whatever it was, the power struggle between the two of them was like an aphrodisiac for Connor. And he had a feeling it was the same for Grae.

"Thank you," Connor said, his voice a bit ragged. Which, of course, had nothing to do with the sudden swell of his cock in his jeans. Nope, nothing to do with that.

The commanding authority that emanated from this man turned him on. It wasn't only physical power, either. The man had intelligence and wisdom. He was no dumb jock.

"Are you hard for me?" Grae asked, staring down into his face, one eyebrow cocked. Grae placed a palm on the wall on each side of Connor's head, leaning in even closer.

Connor stared at Grae's broad lips, remembering how they felt when they were wrapped around his cock. It had been a week since he'd had sex with Grae and Paige. And even though he'd gotten off last night while watching them fuck, it wasn't the same.

Never the same. He had missed their touch, the feel of their skin, their scents.

"Connor, you didn't answer my question." Grae's words were almost a growl, and his eyes held a look of promise.

Connor pulled one of Grae's hands off of the wall and placed it over the bulge in his jeans. "What do you think?"

Grae's fingers cupped him firmly. "I think you're ready for me to fuck you."

The blood rushed to Connor's head. They hadn't gone that far yet. Grae had been preparing him, and Connor knew it was only a matter of time, but...

Grae wanted to take him. A bit of fear of the unknown swept through him. Connor figured he would have no chance of ever topping Grae unless Grae made him his first.

"Have you been doing what I've instructed?" Grae's lips were barely above his.

One shift and they would make contact. Kissing Grae felt so different than kissing his wife. Paige's lips were soft and pliable. Grae's were firm and demanding, like he was. "Yes," Connor answered softly.

"How long did you go?"

Excitement made Connor tremble. "Over six hours."

"When?"

"Today," Connor murmured.

Grae inhaled a deep breath. "When did you remove it?"

"I haven't."

Grae crushed his lips to Connor's, who gasped at the ferocity of the kiss. The other man's tongue moved hungrily into his mouth, exploring the insides, taking control. Connor moaned, his erection becoming even harder, his balls tightening as Grae pinned him against the wall.

Grae's cock was a steel rod against him and Connor wondered what it would be like to finally have it deep inside him, instead of the anal plug that was currently there.

He'd done what Grae had instructed, using the anal plug on a daily basis, extending the time, surprised to find that he really enjoyed the stretching, the fullness it gave him. And every time he had inserted it, the anticipation of Grae finally taking him increased. Back on Grae's boat, he was worried about it. Now, he couldn't wait to experience it.

"I thought about you all week," Grae said, his breathing heavy. "Thought about you going through your work day with the plug in. And now…now I can't wait to have you."

Connor became a little dizzy as heat rushed through him.

Then Paige was there, her face flushed, her eyes full of need. Her hands cupped each one of their cheeks. "I want to see you two kiss again. You don't even know what that did to me."

Connor could imagine how wet Paige was, ready for one or both of them to make her cry out and come.

Connor gripped the back of Grae's smooth head and pulled him down for another kiss. He caught Grae's bottom lip between his teeth and tugged before releasing it and running his tongue over the man's lips.

Grae jerked away but only enough to breathe, "You're playing with fire, Connor. I may have to fuck you right here in the kitchen, against this wall." Then with a sudden move, he twisted Connor around and pushed him against the wall.

Connor's heart was about to beat out of his chest. He braced his hands on the wall as Grae thrust against his ass.

"*Jesus*, Grae," Paige whispered.

Connor turned his head to see her.

She had her bottom lip snagged in her teeth, and she appeared to be using the wall to hold herself up.

He understood the feeling.

"Should I strip your husband right here and show you how ready he is for me?" Grae's breath brushed against Connor's ear, making him shiver.

"Right here, Connor?" Paige asked him.

Before Connor could answer her, Grae barked, "Don't ask him. I'm asking you, Paige."

She looked over at Connor with uncertainty.

Connor didn't know himself what he wanted at the moment. Here? In bed? Did it really matter? But he could see the concern on Paige's face because she knew it would be his first time. He actually wouldn't mind Paige, or even Grae, making the decision instead.

"Bedroom."

Her voice was so soft, Connor wasn't sure if he'd imagined it.

"I want you to take him into the shower. I want you to wash each other. Help him remove the plug, Paige. Get him ready for me."

Connor swallowed hard and nodded. His anticipation was about to be over.

Paige took his hand, squeezing it tight, and as soon as Grae released him from the wall, she led Connor back to the bedroom and into the master bathroom.

She closed the door and turned to face him. "Are you sure you're ready for this?"

God, he loved his wife. She was beautiful, smart, and open-minded—the complete package for him. They had fallen in love so easily, almost instantly. When he met her, he knew she was his other half. And here they were trying to fit someone else in. Even though they had discussed this for a long time, the reality was here now that Grae had moved in almost two weeks ago. This wasn't just a sexual fling with a third person. Everyone was taking it seriously.

He wasn't going to deny it, there were moments when he had doubts about this whole thing. How could he not? Though now as he stood in the bathroom with Paige while they both removed their clothes, he thought about how they'd both been immediately attracted to Grae, even from across the room that night. He realized how lucky they had been that he'd been not only willing to try to become a threesome and not just in bed but in life.

Time would tell how the dynamics of their relationship would evolve. But for now, life was good with his wife. But it was even better with Grae as part of it too.

"Connor?"

Oh yeah, she had asked a question. Paige now stood in front of him naked. He ran his gaze from her long, dark hair at the top of her head down to her cute, polished toenails. It was strange how his brain and body could be so turned on by such feminine features, curves, and softness, while at the same time, also by a man's hard planes and lines, heavy muscle, and the complete male, domineering attitude.

He slid a hand along her jawline, drawing her close enough to press a kiss softly against her lips. "Don't worry. I'm ready. I want this."

She gave him a tentative smile.

He gave her a grin to assure her. "Now, let's get in the shower and maybe you can help me get the plug out. I'm still trying to get the hang of all this."

Paige giggled as she opened the glass shower door and turned on the water, adjusting the temperature.

"Oh, you laugh, but seriously this has been quite an experience."

"Did it turn you on to have it in there?"

Connor watched the muscles in her back shift as she ran a hand under the spray of the water, making sure it wasn't too hot or too cold. "Fuck yes. It was weird at first, but then I really liked it once I relaxed and stopped worrying."

Turning back to face him, her expression looked serious this time. She lowered her voice to below the sound of the shower. "Connor, tell me the truth. Do you mind that he's so demanding?"

Connor felt surprised she was asking this now, of all times. Shouldn't it have been addressed before him moving in if she was concerned? "No, Paige. I honestly don't mind it. I thought I might. But so far, I'm okay."

"Even with that little shit show in the kitchen?"

"It was more a turn-on than anything, baby. Really. Don't worry. I will step in and say something if it goes past my limit."

She nodded and stepped into the shower.

He followed her, closing the shower door behind him. But her question had him thinking. "What about you? You're a strong, independent woman. That's one thing I love about you. Does it bother you?"

Paige shook her head. She'd put her hair up in a bun and tried to avoid the direct spray of the water.

Connor moved under the showerhead. He let the warm water soothe his tight muscles, and he tried to relax his sphincter in preparation for removing the plug.

Paige grabbed the shower pouf and squeezed some gel onto it, then worked it to full lather. She ran it over his shoulders and down his chest. It had been a while since they'd showered together and Connor missed this closeness of washing each other, caring for each other.

"Do you need to squat down or something?"

Connor couldn't help but laugh. "I don't know. This one is larger than the one I started out with. I hope it's easier coming out than it was going in. But I doubt it. And I swear I used a whole bottle of lube."

"Poor baby. Do you want me to help?"

"Yes, because you removing a big latex toy from my ass is so romantic."

Laughing, she swirled the soapy shower pouf over his hips and down his thighs. "Well, your cock hasn't quit since we left the kitchen."

Yeah, it hadn't softened at all since Grae pinned him against the wall. It was kind of getting uncomfortable, especially looking at his wife naked, all slick with water. He imagined himself sliding into her wet heat. He wondered what it would be like fucking her with the plug in.

Damn. They may have to try that.

Though, Connor doubted it would happen at this moment,

because Grae was waiting and what Grae wanted, Grae got. He chuckled.

"What's funny?" Paige asked.

He shook his head. "Nothing. Everything. Okay, I guess I need to figure out how to get this thing out."

"Do you want Grae to come in and remove it? I'm assuming he has more experience with these things than we do."

She was probably right, but no…He wanted to do it himself. Then again, maybe she had a point.

She sucked in a breath to yell out Grae's name, but at the same moment the frosted glass door opened and he stood there.

His dark skin glistened from the steam in the bathroom. "Is there a reason why I'm waiting so long?" he asked, taking in the scene before him.

"Yes," Paige giggled. "Connor needs your help."

Grae raised his eyebrows and gazed at Connor, waiting for the explanation.

"A little advice would be nice," Connor added. He should be embarrassed about the whole situation, but he wasn't. The guy was about to get up close and intimate with his ass anyway, so who cared if the man had to help him out in order to get there.

Then Grae threw his head back and let out the loudest belly laugh.

Connor looked over at Paige, and she stared back at him in surprise and then they both joined in.

"I can't fit in the shower with both of you, so either you guys need to take care of business or, Paige, you need to step out."

Paige began to step out but then stopped. "I want to do it. Just talk us through it."

"It's not rocket science," Grae said, laughter still in his voice.

"I know, but I don't want to hurt him."

"Paige, just go slow. If you think that toy is going to hurt him, then what do you think I'm going to do to him?"

She hesitated and shot a glance at Connor.

Well, he hadn't thought of that until just now, so his confidence about having anal sex with Grae just dropped about a hundred points.

Shit.

"Ah, hell," Grae mumbled. "Connor, face me. Relax."

Connor had no idea why Grae would think giving him the "relax" command would help his body actually relax. But he tried to get into the mindset, telling his muscles to soften, his breathing to slow.

"Kiss me," Grae demanded.

Connor leaned out of the shower enough to meet Grae's lips.

Grae reached down and wrapped his fingers around Connor's still-hard cock, stroking it slowly. Connor groaned against the other man's lips, his mind going from the situation at hand to what Grae did to him instead. Grae worked his tongue into Connor's mouth, while his hands worked their magic, playing with his cock, cupping his balls and lightly squeezing.

Paige's hands stroked along his back and over his buttocks, her hands slippery with shower gel. The more Connor relaxed, the lower she went, stroking the skin along his cheeks and then in between them. He felt her hook the latex ring with her fingers and slightly pull. But his body resisted, tightening up.

Grae bit his bottom lip, causing Connor to gasp and while he was distracted, Paige worked the plug out.

Connor moaned at the feeling of the stretch and the small pinch-like pain, but then he suddenly felt very empty. Way too empty.

Grae pulled away, brushing a thumb over the small cut in Connor's lip. "Don't worry, I'll be inside you soon." He reached in to shut the water off, and they both climbed out of the shower, grabbing towels to dry off. "I'll be waiting for you in bed," he said, his smile a bit crooked as he walked out of the bathroom.

Connor couldn't help but watch the flex of the other man's muscles as he left.

When he and Paige entered the bedroom, Grae was in bed, waiting for them, as he said. There were condoms and a bottle of lube on the bedside stand also at the ready.

Though, Grae wasn't smiling anymore.

His nostrils flared, and he watched them both closely as they approached. He looked animalistic, ready to pounce, as he leaned back against the headboard, his gaze pinned on them.

A thrill shot through Connor.

Paige climbed onto the bed, crawling up to Grae's side. He didn't look at her. He only had eyes for Connor.

Connor grabbed himself and stroked his length. His erection was harder than ever. He wanted to sink into Paige's softness but also wanted to feel Grae deep inside him.

Was it possible to do both at the same time? He sure as hell hoped so. "I want to fuck Paige as you're fucking me." Connor still stood at the end of the bed gazing at his two lovers. He couldn't imagine either would say no to his suggestion.

Grae's gaze flicked to Paige and then back to him. "We can do that."

Just the thought of it made Connor want to lose his load. He closed his eyes for a moment and sucked in a breath. He needed to keep his shit together. Tonight was a major step for him, and he needed to keep his head on straight.

"Connor…" Paige lifted a hand to him. "I want your face between my thighs, while I take Grae in my mouth."

Connor just about leaped onto the bed. Paige shifted and slid down the mattress. Connor gripped her thighs, pulling them apart and without hesitation, tasted the sweet goodness of his wife.

She was already slick and hot; her folds silky and plump as his tongue worked in and out of her. He flicked the tip against her clit, making her hips jump off the bed. Her thighs clenched around his ears for a moment before releasing. He looked up the line of her body to see Grae's broad back to him. He straddled her body, and though he couldn't see it, he could imagine Grae's long, hard length in her mouth as she sucked him.

Connor slid two fingers inside her core, feeling her muscles tighten around his digits, trying to pull him deeper. He swirled his tongue around her sensitive button, making it twitch while her hips danced. Her moans were muffled with Grae keeping her mouth full. He could see Grae's buttocks flex as he pushed his cock in and out of her.

Connor sucked on her swollen flesh as he curved his fingers to find that spot of hers. The one that made her gush and cry out when he caressed it. With his lips sucking her clit and his digits deep inside her, a climax broke over her. He could feel the wet heat making her even slicker and ready for his cock to be inside her. Drops of precum beaded at the head of his erection.

He didn't think he could wait much longer as he moved up the bed only to see Grae's hands gripping Paige's hair tightly as he fucked her mouth. Tears rolled from the corners of her eyes because of how deep she took him…But she didn't tap out. She accepted every inch of him.

Grae's eyes were closed, and his head tilted back as he pulled her head up to meet each thrust. Small sounds at the back of her throat brought his attention back to her face. He softened the hold on her hair, then released her completely, shifting his hips back until only the head of his cock was between her lips. "I want to come in your wife's mouth, but I'm saving it all for you." He turned his eyes toward Connor. "Are you ready?"

"Yes." Yes, he felt more than fucking ready. Connor was about to explode.

Grae laid a kiss on Paige's forehead before rolling away to grab the lube and a condom from the top of the nightstand.

"I love you, baby," Connor whispered to Paige before kissing her and settling over top of her.

She smiled up at him. "I love you too."

He dropped his head and captured one of her puckered, pink

nipples into his mouth, grazing the tip with his teeth. Her back arched as he tugged on one with his lips, the other with his fingers. He brushed kisses along the outer swells of her breasts, murmuring against her skin about how good this was going to feel.

The bed shifted as Grae moved behind him, the man's fingers suddenly gripping his hips.

Connor turned his head to look behind him. Then for a second, he almost had second thoughts as he took in Grae's length and girth encased in latex and lube.

"You're going to do what I tell you, Connor."

Yes, of course, the man had more experience when it came to these sexual escapades than he did, so it only made sense to follow the big guy's lead.

"Tell me you heard me."

"Yes, I heard you," he told Grae.

With a sharp nod of his head, Grae moved closer, the heat and hard length of Grae's cock pressed against his crease. Just the feel of the other man against his skin made him want to push back, to invite his entry. But he waited. Grae knew what he was doing.

The cool lube trickled over his anus and down the crease of his ass. Connor bit back a gasp, and he turned back to look at his wife lying beneath him. Her pupils were dilated as she watched his face, his expressions, her gaze sometimes flicking back to Grae.

Fingers firmly distributed the lube in circles around his tight entrance, pressing gently, encouraging him to open, to accept Grae. Since using the anal plugs, the pressure and the stretch from Grae's finger penetrating him didn't feel as foreign. It felt good, and he wanted more. He was ready for more than a finger or two. He was ready to have the man take him completely.

Grae eased two fingers in and out of him, adding lube, preparing him for what was coming next. "God, you're still so tight," he said, sounding tense.

It wasn't Grae asking him if he was ready. It was Paige. And when he answered her, he stared into her eyes as Grae pressed the head of his cock against him, opening him up. Connor suddenly wanted to surge back against him.

Grae held his hips like a vise. "Don't move. Let me," was all that he said.

Paige no longer looked at him but watched Grae. For a moment, Connor wished he could see Grae too. He could imagine the look of ecstasy the man wore as he pushed slowly into Connor's tight canal.

Once Grae pushed past the tight ring, Connor relaxed even more, the feeling of fullness overtaking him. Though, the man still had more length to go.

When Grae was finally fully seated, he let out a sound.

The guttural sound coming from the back of his throat made Connor even harder. The pressure against his prostate made him close his eyes. It was odd but amazing at the same time to have Grae a part of him.

You couldn't make any more of a connection with another person without having a part of them inside of you.

His heart pounded in his chest, and he opened his eyes to look down at Paige.

Her eyes were hooded, her cheeks flushed, and she had both nipples between her fingers as she twisted them. "I want you inside me now, baby," she said to him.

Oh, how he wanted that too.

"Not yet," Grae warned. His words sounded like they came from between clenched teeth.

Grae slowly withdrew, but not completely. Then he moved forward again, just as slow.

Connor had only got a glimpse of how good this would feel with the plug and now that Grae was inside him, he couldn't believe the pleasure another man could give him. "Fuck me," Connor encouraged him, wanting him to move faster.

"I need…to go…slow." Grae panted as he tried to speak. "Give it…a moment."

It was good to know the man had a weakness… something he could lose his tight control over. Anal sex must be his Kryptonite.

Though Connor wanted to smile over his discovery, he couldn't because Grae decided to pick up the pace. And none-so-gently either.

Grae held Connor's hips in place as he fucked him hard, skin slapping against skin.

Connor cried out, his fingers digging into the sheets. The urge to come felt so strong, and Connor found that crazy. But he didn't want to come. Not yet. He wanted to come while inside Paige. He tried to catch his breath to tell Grae, but he couldn't. Each thrust of Grae's hips made him grunt instead.

After what seemed like an eternity, but, in reality, was only seconds, Grae slowed, letting his fingers relax along Connor's hips. "Carefully lower your hips, Connor. Fuck your wife."

Grae held their connection as Connor lowered himself carefully between Paige's thighs. She'd bent her knees and helped guide him inside her. And when he was surrounded by her wet heat, he almost lost it.

It was just as he'd imagined. Her softness, his hardness. The urge to thrust into her became strong.

"You control the movement, Connor."

Then suddenly what Grae said made sense.

With every push and pull of Connor's hips, he fucked Paige, while Grae fucked him. For once, Connor had all of the control. The harder he fucked his wife, the harder Grae fucked him.

Until Connor's head was spinning. He was on the edge of losing it.

Paige squirmed underneath him, encouraging him to fuck her faster, harder. Her hips bucking against him. Her own fingers found her clit and circled it, pressed it, pushed it until finally, she surged against him, calling out.

Her core rippled around him, squeezing and releasing his cock like a fist.

Then like her, he shattered, his cock pulsing deep inside her, his most intense release ever.

Above him, Grae grunted one last time before becoming still, his cock pulsing deep inside Connor.

And with that, the three of them were finally one.

CHAPTER 9

Paige woke up in a tangle of legs, which was not surprising. But what *was* surprising was she hadn't woken up in the middle. For the first time since Grae had moved in, he slept in between her and Connor.

When she lifted her head, she almost expected to see them spooning. But they weren't. Grae laid flat on his back, taking up most of the bed space. He tended to be a bed hog. And it wasn't like the bed wasn't big enough.

When he'd moved in, they decided to put two queen mattresses together. However, it could still be a tight fit with Sir Hog-A-Bed-A-Lot.

Before she could slide quietly from between the sheets to relieve her full bladder, a dark arm snaked around her and pulled her tight against him.

"Where do you think you're going?" His voice sounded rough from sleep and it sent a shiver down her spine.

"To pee."

With a slight nod of his head, Grae released her. "Hurry back."

She did as she was told not because she wasn't going to do it anyway, she was actually still exhausted from last night's activities and could use more sleep and cuddle time.

When she crawled back under the covers, she hooked a thigh over Grae's tree-trunk of a leg. She laid her head on his chest and let out a long, satisfied smile.

"Happy?" His words rumbled through his chest to her ear.

"Yes."

"Why?" he asked.

An odd question and she wasn't sure how to answer it. Analyzing her happiness wasn't something she did first thing in the morning. But she truly did feel happy.

Maybe the answer was as simple as the two men lying in the same bed as her. Maybe it was the ache between her legs from all the different ways they had gotten each other off last night. Maybe it was the thought that her husband finally got what he'd fantasized about for so long but had been too afraid to go after.

Maybe.

"I just am." She peered up at his face. "How about you? Are you happy?"

"Yes," he answered.

Short and to the point, not that she expected more, but she would ask anyway. "Why?"

"I just am," he echoed, a smile breaking the seriousness of his expression.

She smiled back, tracing her fingers around his short, thick goatee. "You know, I hate facial hair."

He cocked an eyebrow. "Really?"

She lifted her shoulders slightly. "Yeah. Never liked it on guys. But it fits you."

He grabbed her fingers and brought them to his lips to brush a light kiss along their tips. "Does it?"

"Hmm. You're like the black version of Mr. Clean with your gold hoop earring and all."

He chuckled. "Mr. Clean doesn't have a goatee."

"Meh. Maybe he should."

Connor stretched and yawned on the other side of Grae.

Paige lifted her head slightly off of Grae's chest to look at her husband. "How are you feeling this morning?"

Connor frowned, skooched around a bit, then rolled to his side to look at them. His shaggy hair looked like a wild mess.

Paige felt tempted to reach out and smooth it.

"A bit sore."

"To be expected," Grae said.

"I had a dream last night. I figured out what my deepest, darkest fantasy is. Only mine isn't deep." He yawned again and rubbed his eyes. "Or dark, actually."

Paige had almost forgotten about the question Grae had posed to them on the boat. She hadn't given it much thought, and Grae hadn't bugged for her answer. "Well?" She prodded him.

"*Weeell*, I want to have sex in public," Connor answered.

"All three of us?" It was risky for two people to have sex in public and not get caught. But three? Paige wondered if it was possible.

"In my dream we were, yes. But we were on a stage in front of an audience."

"Like a sex show?" she asked.

Connor shrugged. "I guess so. It was a dream. It's not like I had all the details."

"I doubt we'll be having sex in front of an audience," Grae finally said.

Oddly enough, it was Grae who ended up smoothing down Connor's hair. Connor acted like it was a normal thing between the two of them and Paige opened her mouth to mention it but shut it since there was no reason to point it out. The men seemed much closer after last night, and she didn't want to draw attention to it in case they became self-conscious. Mentally, she shook her head. Self-consciousness and Graedon Ward did not go together. Silly her. What was she thinking?

"No. But maybe we can pull it off somehow," Connor said. "I mean, we don't need to be watched, right? It's the thrill of being caught that's the excitement."

"Like having sex on the beach?" Paige suggested.

"No. I've had sex on the beach. I won't be doing that again," Connor said. "Damp skin, sand, friction, and sensitive parts don't go together very well."

"I can imagine," Grae murmured. "There's always the bow of the boat."

"In the marina," Connor added.

"Yeah, if you want to be arrested, honey," Paige said, frowning. "That's a big fat no."

"We can figure something out," Grae told him. He turned his gaze down to her, still laying on his chest. "And you? Have you thought about what your deepest, darkest fantasy is?"

"No. But I will. What about you?"

"I'll reveal mine at the right time," he answered.

Really? So, he had a fantasy that had to be told at the right moment? *Interesting.* A blaring ringtone made Paige jump. She didn't recognize it, so she knew it wasn't her phone.

No one moved for a moment, but then Connor grabbed the offending cell and passed it over to Grae. "Yours," he said.

Grae frowned, staring at the Caller-ID.

Paige thought he would let it go to voicemail, but he swiped at the screen at the last second, giving the person on the other end a gruff greeting.

She felt guilty listening to the one-sided conversation, but Grae's short answers and questions really didn't give anything away. If Grae wanted privacy, he could excuse himself from the bed, but the conversation was over in minutes.

Connor's eyes had drifted closed again. Although apparently, he wasn't actually asleep because he held out his hand for Grae's phone, and then without a word, put it back on the nightstand.

Paige was dying to ask Grae who would call him on an early

Saturday morning but knew him being such a private a man, he probably wouldn't appreciate the nosiness.

"Well," Grae started, pushing himself up to a seated position to prop himself against the headboard. As he moved, Paige's head had slipped into his lap, and he now tangled his fingers into her hair, while his thumb stroked her ear.

Paige never realized how much ears were an erogenous zone. Not until Grae. No man had ever caressed, licked, or sucked her there. Not even Connor.

"Well," Grae continued. "My sister is going to be in town next weekend. And she would like to get together with me."

"Which one?" Paige asked, remembering that he had three siblings and Grae was the oldest out of all four.

"The youngest, Gia. However, here's the thing. She's bringing my sister and brother along for a visit. Apparently, I've been neglecting my family, and since I don't go to visit them, they have all decided to come here."

"Here? To this house?" Paige asked, surprised they would even know about her or Connor.

He shook his head. "No. To my house. They'll be arriving Friday night and staying the weekend."

Paige couldn't tell if he felt happy or angry about the unexpected visit. He didn't talk about his family or their dynamics. And she hadn't bothered to ask. She knew she would get his typical short answers or none at all. Paige was learning to let him tell them things at his own pace. Every once in a while, he would reveal a piece of his complex puzzle. Usually, when you least expected it.

"So basically, you're saying that you'll be back at your house next weekend doing your family thing. Not a problem," Connor said, burrowing deeper under the covers and plumping a pillow for under his head.

"No, that's not what I'm saying. That's what *you're* saying," Grae answered.

"Wait," Paige said. "Is there a holiday I'm missing, one I don't know about? Why now?"

"I was told it worked out between their schedules and since I'm not traveling this month for recruiting, it was a good time. Though, they conveniently forgot to ask me how I felt about the whole thing." Grae sounded a bit bitter.

Now she really wondered what his relationship was like with his family. "It'll only be for a couple of days, Grae. We'll survive without you for that long, won't we, honey?" Paige asked Connor.

Before Connor could answer, Grae spoke, "No. You'll be coming with me." He glanced at Connor and then back at Paige. "Both of you."

Paige's eyebrows shot to her hairline. She pushed off his lap to sit up, wrapping a corner of the sheet around her. "Do you think that's a good idea?"

"Should I hide our relationship from my family?"

Good question. Her brother was the only family she had, and he knew about their arrangement. But then he's the one who started this whole thing. His polyamory relationship and love life showed Paige that a successful threesome was possible.

So, of course, Logan had no problem with it. Or he'd be a hypocrite.

"No, I guess not. But it's one thing to tell them about it…it's another thing to shove it in their face when they aren't expecting it."

"I'm not shoving anything in their face. If it were just you and me, Paige, I'd expect you to be by my side when my family visits. And vice versa. And if I was gay and Connor was my sole partner, I'd handle it the same way."

A thumbs up came from beneath the pile of covers on Connor's side of the bed.

"Does your family even know you're bi-sexual?" Paige realized he never once had used the bisexual label in regards to his sexuality. But that's what he was, and society was going to label him, whether he liked it or not.

"I'm sure they do," he murmured.

No, she wasn't convinced yet. "Have you actually told them, though?"

"It's not a thing that you normally bring up at a family brunch, Paige."

Maybe he was right. Logan never actually announced he was bisexual. He just fell in love with Ty and Ty became a part of his life. In fact, Paige had thought Logan was gay, not bisexual, for the longest time. It wasn't until he brought Quinn into his already established relationship that the light dawned on Paige that her brother was bi. Not that she ever cared. She only ever wanted her brother to be happy. Especially after the rough start to his life.

Ty had made Logan a better person. And she loved Ty like a brother and Quinn like a sister, proving family wasn't always blood.

"You have to treat our relationship like any other relationship," Grae said, he grabbed her wrist and brought it to his lips. The tip of his tongue tickled her skin there, and she relaxed a little, settling back along his side. "There's no reason for us to hide even if our relationship is atypical."

"I never said I wanted to hide it," Paige said.

"Are you nervous about meeting my family?" he asked her.

"No, not nervous. More like anxious about how they are going to react. But really, isn't any new girlfriend or boyfriend nervous to meet their new beau's family?"

Grae chuckled at her use of "beau." "I suppose you're right. I might be a bit anxious when meeting Connor's family for the first time."

At the mention of his name, Connor peeked his head out from under the covers. "Uh, that isn't going to happen anytime soon. They're all back in Australia. And they're not so open-minded.

Believe me. In fact, they weren't happy when I married a crazy American."

Paige grabbed a pillow from behind her and reached over Grae to whack Connor. "Crazy American. *Please.* They were happy when I took you away. And your family loves me."

Connor made a sound as he ducked under the covers again to avoid another strike of the pillow. Laughing, his two hands came out in surrender. "If you bruise me, baby, I'll introduce myself to his siblings as your sex slave."

Paige laughed. "That would really have their heads spinning."

Paige's head was spinning. Enough so, that the sound of the doorbell made her jump out of her skin. She bit her bottom lip as she wrung her hands.

This would be the first time their new relationship was on display to strangers. Well, strangers to her and Connor, anyway.

Grae scowled at her until she released her lip. "Calm down. You're making this a much bigger deal than it is."

"Whatever, Mr. Cool-Calm-and-Collected."

He shook his head and walked to the front entry to let his guests, aka siblings, in.

Paige waited—more like hid—in the kitchen wondering where the hell Connor was. Grae's house was much bigger than theirs, and she had a hard time keeping track of where the men were sometimes.

A mixture of voices rose and fell from the front entryway, and Paige thought she might pass out at any moment. Her heart pounded, and she felt surprised she wasn't in a cold sweat already.

She could hear Grae doing his host duties, helping them with their luggage, and whatever else they needed assistance with.

She still had time to slip out the back and run away. But she froze in place instead as what sounded like a herd of noisy humans came closer. She gripped the counter for support and pasted a stiff smile on her face. She hoped it looked at least a little bit genuine.

It slipped a little as his first sister walked into the kitchen.

Holy fuck, where were they from? The Amazon?

His sister—Paige didn't know which one—was *tall*. And beautiful. Her dark skin and makeup were flawless. Her black hair long and straight. And she had curves that didn't quit in an outfit that was impeccably stylish.

Paige felt suddenly conscious of how casually she was dressed.

The woman stopped short when she saw Paige and let out a little "Oh!" She looked back over her shoulder and said, "Grae, there's a white woman in your kitchen. Is she the housekeeper?"

What remained of Paige's smile fell flat. In fact, it fell so far, it turned into a frown.

Housekeeper?

Grae's deep chuckle came from down the hallway.

He ushered the rest of his family into the kitchen, and they all lined up staring at her like they've never seen a woman before. Or maybe a woman in Grae's house. Which made her shoot him a glance.

He gave her a twisted smile. Well, she was glad Grae found this amusing because she didn't like being on display like an animal in a zoo.

Grae stepped forward to stand by Paige's side. "Well, Gayle, you're right about one thing. She's a white woman. That's hard to miss. But she's not my housekeeper. In fact, she doesn't like to clean up dirt; she plays with it instead." He leaned over and kissed Paige on the lips.

Paige didn't kiss him back. She simply stood there blinking, her eyes not leaving the lineup of his two sisters and brother. They were *all* tall. Between their similar skin tone and facial features, as well as their height, she could easily see they were related.

"Paige, these are my incorrigible siblings, and I hope they don't scare you away."

"I don't scare easily," Paige muttered.

"That's good because that's not my sisters' intent. Right, ladies?" Grae's brother said, stepping forward. He held out his hand.

They could be twins, Grae and this nameless brother. The biggest differences were his hair being tightly trimmed to this head, no facial hair, and wasn't anywhere near as built as Grae. He was slimmer, but still looked in very good shape, and just as handsome. And it appeared they were the exact same height.

"I'm Gryff."

Interesting name.

Grae's brother shook his head, still holding out his hand, waiting for Paige to accept it. "Gryffin Ward. Gryff for short," he corrected.

Paige shook his hand. It was as broad and strong as Grae's. "You could be twins," she murmured.

"Don't get any ideas," Grae said under his breath before introducing his two sisters.

Gayle, the sister who had entered the kitchen first, was in the middle age-wise, sort of, because it was hard to be in the middle with four children. She had to be at least six inches taller than her. Paige guessed she was in her late twenties, but couldn't be sure. Grae's other sister was introduced as Gia. If she were an inch shorter than Gayle, Paige would be surprised. The women were curvy, for sure, and absolutely stunning. Their family had been a winner in the gene pool. Well, except for the heart condition that had plagued Grae.

Gia seemed to warm up to Paige quicker than Gayle, who stood back a bit, reserved. Paige took it to be because Gia was the youngest of the bunch.

She approached the two of them and gave Paige a hug in

greeting and then punched Grae in the arm. "Big brother, why didn't you tell us that you had a girlfriend?"

Heat flamed up Paige's cheeks. *If only it were that simple.*

"Since when has Grae volunteered any personal information about his life to us?" Gayle asked, sounding a little perturbed about it.

"It's always been like pulling teeth to get any news from him. Why are you surprised?" Gryff asked, giving Paige a smile and a wink as if she could commiserate.

Yeah, she could.

Grae laid an arm around Paige's shoulder and pulled her against his side. "Now you know," was all he said.

Typical Grae.

Gia laughed and shook her head. "Well, I, for one, am glad to see you, big brother. I've missed you. And I'm glad you're getting laid." She bounced on her toes. "But I need the little girl's room. Please point the way." She disappeared back the way they had come.

The rest of them stood looking at each other, a bit uncomfortable until Grae made a move. "Why don't we head into the living room so we can all relax before dinner."

"That sounds like a plan," Gryff agreed, evidently ready to break the awkwardness.

Grae handed Paige a couple bottles of wine, then he picked up a tray of stemmed glasses and they all trooped into the living room. He'd already set up trays of cheese and crackers around the room and lit the gas fireplace, though more for the ambiance than for warmth since it was late in the season for a fire.

Paige waited for Grae's brother and sister to pick spots to settle into around the room. They migrated to the loveseat and recliner leaving Grae and Paige the sofa.

Then before she could move to the couch, Gia rushed in, dragging Connor behind her. "I found this one down the hall. Does he belong to anyone?" She beamed at Connor, and he returned the smile. She unmistakably batted her eyelashes at him. "Because if he doesn't, then I'm going to keep him. He's got the cutest accent."

"He's not a stray kitten, Gia," Grae said.

His youngest sister laughed and shrugged. "It's not finders, keepers? Well, it was worth a shot."

"Are there any other people just wandering around your house that we should be aware of?" Gayle asked.

"No. That should be the last one. Connor, you've already met my little sister, Gia. The one with the stick up her ass over there is Gayle, and that's my brother Gryffin."

"Gryff," his brother corrected, rising from his seat just enough to reach out and shake hands with Connor.

"This is Connor Morgan. Paige's husband."

Gryff's chair complained loudly when he dropped abruptly back into it, a stunned look on his face.

"Damn, he *is* taken," Gia said, disappointed, not joining in on her older siblings' shock.

"Yes, sorry, I am," Connor said, acting like he could care less about the bomb Grae just dropped. He moved to the sideboard and started to pour the wine.

Paige envied his easiness about the whole situation. In contrast, she felt like a deer caught in headlights. In any case, she guessed there wasn't an easy way to explain their relationship. Better just to rip off the Band-Aid.

"Grae…" Gayle started, a frown on her face.

"Connor, can you give my sister a glass of wine? She looks like she needs it."

Gayle accepted the wineglass and took a sip. And then another.

"So wait… What am I missing?" Gia asked, standing in the center of the room, her glass halfway to her lips. "I thought Paige was your girlfriend?"

Paige hated the term girlfriend because it sounded so sophomoric. Plus, she felt sure Grae disliked it too.

"Something like that," Grae murmured, settling on the couch to face his siblings.

Grae reached his hand out to Paige, and she took it. He pulled her towards the couch, encouraging her to sit next to him. She did, though she felt a little uncomfortable about it with Gayle across the way staring at them, obviously not a happy camper.

Gryff seemed to be taking the disclosure in stride.

Gia appeared to have too many thoughts wanting to escape her head. So different from her oldest brother. She gazed over at Paige. "So your husband doesn't mind you sleeping with my brother?"

"I don't mind," Connor said casually, putting the now empty wine bottle back on the table.

"Damn, that makes you even cuter," she said, sidling up to Connor and touching his arm. "So open-minded."

Paige didn't miss the lingering brush of her fingers, and neither did Grae, whose muscles tensed.

Connor gave her another smile, then moved away to sit to Paige's right.

"So, do you take turns?"

"Seriously, Gia, we're not going to sit here and dissect their sex life," Gryff said.

"But I'm curious."

"Curiosity killed the cat," Gryff reminded her.

Grae lifted a hand, indicating that he would handle the matter. "I understand your curiosity, Gia. It's to be expected."

"So, tell me," she encouraged.

"It's simple. We're all lovers."

Her gaze bounced off each of them, one by one. "At the same time?"

"Yes."

"Damn," she whispered in amazement, her eyes all lit up. "I'd join in if you weren't my brother."

"But I am, and I don't even want that image in my head. So, please, sit down, drink your wine, and have some cheese."

"Which means the subject is closed," Gryff clarified to their youngest sister.

"I know what it means, Gryff. Jeez." Gia pouted as she took herself and her wine to the seat closest to the fire, curling up into a recliner. "But just one more question…"

"No," Grae said loud and firmly.

Paige sighed in relief. She didn't realize she had Grae's hand locked in hers and had been squeezing the shit out of it.

She relaxed her grip, and he gave her a pained smile.

Luckily, Connor was laid-back and social enough that he could start a conversation with a rock, so he got the small talk going about what everyone did for a living, as well as all the niceties and blah-blah-blahs like that. Anything to deflect the conversation from their unusual relationship.

Except, of course, every time Gia could interject, she tried her damnedest to bring the conversation back around to anything that concerned the three of them.

"So, what… You all live here?" Gia waved an arm around the room.

Paige was about to correct her, but Grae stopped her by saying, "Yes." His short answer once again, shutting his youngest, most curious sister down.

"How did that work out for you last time?" Gayle asked Grae.

Paige's ears perked. "Last time?" she asked.

Grae shot his sister a killer look, which Paige did not miss.

Gayle held up her palms, saying, "Your life, brother. You deal with it as you wish."

Paige would like to know what "last time" meant. A live-in lover or girlfriend?

Grae was then saved by the bell when the caterer arrived with the dinner he'd ordered.

When the table was set and the food laid out, they wandered into the formal dining room. A room which Paige thought ended up being a waste in most people's home except during large family gatherings.

Grae took the spot at the head of the table after pulling out Paige's chair for her to his right. With a tilt of his head, he indicated Connor should sit to his left. Gryff settled at the other end of the table across from his brother, his sisters flanking him.

Paige stared at the spread on the table and was impressed. Though, she didn't know why. It was Grae. He didn't seem to do anything half-assed. Everything the caterer brought looked too good to eat, and she was glad she didn't have to cook. Her skills were passable enough so Connor and she never starved, but that was her limit.

During dinner, the siblings caught up with each other's lives and also talked about their parents. Paige had to admit she'd learned more about Grae during the small talk than ever before. Grae hadn't really mentioned his parents, and once again, Paige hadn't bothered to pry. Now, with the four G's—what Paige was mentally calling the brothers and sisters—all together, she learned that they had retired a while ago and moved out to Arizona for the dry, warm climate. They revealed their father had been an inventor and had made some inventions he'd sold for beaucoup bucks, so the kids had never wanted for anything.

Paige continued to make mental notes, sometimes glancing up at Grae and lifting a brow. He would ignore her and continue the conversation. Paige just knew that he, like Lucy, had a lot of *splainin'* to do after tonight's dinner.

Most of the conversation across the table was between Grae, Gayle, and Gryff, though an occasional question would be lobbed at Paige. Friendly ones from Gryff, more direct ones from Gayle. For the most part, Paige could understand why Gayle wanted to protect her brother from any kind of hurt, but she found herself losing her patience with Grae's sister.

Since Gia purposely sat next to Connor, they hardly joined in on the conversation as Gia kept his attention on her. Grae's youngest sister seemed to be infatuated with him. By now, the woman probably knew more about Australia than Paige did. When he started in on Australian football, Paige just rolled her eyes and figured Gia would eventually become bored to death. Instead, she hung on every word. Paige felt tempted to go over and check Connor for a hard-on. Not over Gia, but his revered sport of football.

Whatever made him happy. As long as Grae's sister didn't cross any boundaries, Paige let him have his fun. Though, she noticed, Grae seemed to be keeping an eye on them more than she was.

Interesting.

Did becoming Connor's first turn Grae more possessive of his male lover?

Maybe she needed to distract him. Just a bit. She leaned her breasts against his arm as he ate. "Tied up. Spanked. Double teamed," Paige whispered into Grae's ear.

Her words apparently caught Grae off guard, because he croaked, "What?" and his eyes widened for a second.

"You asked what my deepest, darkest fantasy was," she murmured, making sure no one else at the table heard her. She enjoyed watching the King of Cool lose his shit. She would have to remember to do it more often. There was nothing wrong with keeping him on his toes, keeping him guessing.

Grae placed his fork down on his plate carefully and leveled his gaze at her, hesitating a few heartbeats before answering, "I assume all at the same time?"

Paige lifted a shoulder slightly, her blood furiously rushing through her, and her mind spinning as the fantasy played out in her head.

He frowned, picked up his napkin, and pretended to wipe his lips. Hiding his mouth behind the cloth, he whispered, "Revealing that right now with my family in the house is just plain rotten, Paige."

She laughed, sitting back in her seat. "I know. But it just came to me."

"At dinner."

"Yep."

Grae shook his head.

"What's so funny down there?" Grae's brother asked.

Heat rushed to Paige's cheek. Now may not have been the time to admit her fantasy since they couldn't act upon it this weekend, but she just bet Grae was as hard as a rock under the table. Her hand crept over into his lap. *Yep.*

He coughed as she traced her fingers over his length before pulling away.

"Are you okay, big brother?"

Grae picked up his wine and took a sip. "Perfectly fine. Thank you. A bit of food went down the wrong pipe."

Then the conversation turned to the time when their father had to do the Heimlich maneuver on their aunt during Thanksgiving dinner.

Paige peeked over at Grae.

He just stared at her.

Connor, who must have heard at least part of the conversation kept his head down, concentrating on his food, an eager smile on his face. At least until Gia started asking questions about wallabies and kangaroos like he was some zoologist.

I s it kinda like sister wives?"

Paige jumped, narrowly missing the metal refrigerator shelf with her noggin since she'd been leaning in to grab a bottle of water.

The kitchen had been empty when she had wandered in. Where the hell had Gia been hiding?

Paige straightened, shut the fridge door, and regarded Grae's youngest sister. Gia was like a dog with a bone. She wasn't going to let it go anytime soon. "I don't think sister wives sleep together," Paige replied, unsure if she should be amused with this obsession or annoyed. Though she imagined it would be highly entertaining to introduce her to Logan, Ty, and Quinn, as well as Ren, Cole, and Eve. The woman's head would probably explode.

"I am envious of what you have. This…" Gia waved her hand in the air. "Triangle."

"Do you have a significant other?" Paige asked her, leaning against the kitchen island.

"No, nothing serious." Gia paced past her to the other side of the kitchen. "I'm not ready to settle down." Then she spun sharply on her heel to rush up to Paige. "Does my brother have sex with your husband? Is he gay?"

Paige considered Gia for a moment, before slowly and carefully saying, "He's not gay." And since the woman liked to play twenty questions, it was time to turn the tables. "Do you have any knowledge of this previous relationship Gayle almost let slip?"

Gia bounced on her toes, a sign that her mind must be spinning a million miles a minute, and then she leaned calmly against the counter across from Paige. It was like someone had thrown a switch. "No. But I've been kinda out of the loop while away at college. So, it might have happened then."

"You're not giving away any family secrets, are you?" Grae interrupted, his eyes narrowing as he entered the room. His gaze jumped from Gia to Paige and back.

"If only I knew some to tell," Gia responded, pouting. "I'm always the last to know. It sucks being the baby."

"You're saying that our parents didn't spoil you since you were the baby."

She shrugged.

Paige swore Grae rolled his eyes. Impossible. He didn't do things like that.

Gia's face lit up as if a light bulb suddenly turned on. "Since you're going to go sleep with my brother, can I borrow your husband?"

Paige's jaw dropped. If it weren't scraping the floor, she would be surprised. Did this woman have no boundaries? And all of this came out of her mouth sounding so innocent. Like it was normal to just ask another woman to have sex with her husband.

"Gia, you don't borrow someone's husband."

"Unless you're swingers," Paige murmured, finally picking her jaw off the floor.

Grae shot her a look which seemed to say, *You're not helping.*

"Isn't that what you're doing when you have sex with him?" Gia asked her brother.

"We're not…*swingers*. We're in a relationship," Grae clarified.

With the questions Gia asked, as well as her mannerisms, Paige guessed that she had to be twenty-three or twenty-four years old at the most. Even though she had graduated from college, she acted like a woman a lot younger. But what Gia asked got Paige thinking.

What if Connor *wanted* to have sex with Gia? Would she let him? Did she feel any jealousy at all with the attention Gia gave Connor all evening?

Paige enjoyed having sex with another man and didn't expect any jealousy from her own husband. Should he expect the same from her?

"Even if Connor agreed, Paige would have to," Grae continued, causing Gia to shoot Paige a hopeful look. "And even if Paige agreed, I would have to. And sorry, dear sister, I don't. So, go to bed."

Gia gave him a big, fake pout. "You know I'm going to be up all night thinking about what you three are doing in that over-sized bed of yours."

"I can tell you right now, so you'll be able to get your beauty rest. We're going to be sleeping."

Well, this was news to Paige, but it made sense with his family in the house.

"Why? Are you guys really loud?"

Grae's sister didn't seem to have a filter, and the question just hit her in a way that Paige couldn't help but laugh.

"Goodnight, Gia," Grae said firmly, leaving no room for his sister to believe the conversation was anything but over. He grabbed Paige's arm and steered her out of the room.

"So, are we really going to sleep?" she asked, a little disappointed.

"No."

"You think we can be quiet?" If so, he had more confidence in this possibility than she did.

"That's what gags were made for."

Paige smiled up at him as they approached the stairs. "I like how you think."

"You sure this is what you want?" Gayle asked.

Grae glanced at his sister and then back over at Paige and Connor splashing around in the deep end of the pool. He had turned the heater on, and they had decided to brave the water. Gia decided not to get in, instead lounging in the sun. She wore some expensive looking bikini and designer sunglasses, and always seemed to pose when Connor happened to look her way.

Gryff poked fun at her every time she took a selfie, making

what Grae's brother called duck lips. He'd borrowed a pair of swim trunks and sat at the edge of the pool, swinging his legs in the water while watching Paige and Connor's antics, a smile on his face.

The couple kept drawing everyone's attention. How could they not when every time Connor would dunk his wife, Paige would squeal, laugh, and jump on his back, pretending to beat him up.

Paige wore a little bikini too, and Grae noticed Gryff's gaze kept landing on Paige's nipples which were clearly hard beneath the wet fabric.

Grae's fingers curled into fists, and he blew out a breath. This was his brother, he reminded himself.

"Is it?" Gayle said, waving a hand in front of his face.

"Sorry?" he asked, realizing he was distracted.

"I asked if this is really what you want. Gia and Gryff don't know the whole story, but I do, Grae. The relationship with Joshua and Marla wrecked you."

"I survived, Gayle. I'm fine." His eyes drifted back to the pool. Now in the shallow end, Paige had her arms around Connor's neck and her legs wrapped around his waist as they kissed. Connor's hands were firmly planted on his wife's ass.

"Yes, *now* you're fine. But back then—"

"Drop it, Gayle," he warned, cutting her off. He tore his gaze away from the pool. "Do you want a drink?"

"No. I want you to talk to me."

"I don't want to talk about it, dear sister of mine," he said, frowning. He hoped she would get the hint and drop the subject.

"All weekend I've noticed that they tell each other they love one another. They call each other *honey* and *baby*. And you're just *Grae*."

"I hadn't noticed." Of course he had, but he wasn't going to admit this to his sister.

"Do they even know about your previous…" She waved a well-manicured hand in the air. "Thing?"

"Thing?"

"Your love triangle."

Grae sighed, sat back in his chair, and crossed his ankles. He wanted to correct her and say it wasn't a triangle. But in the end, it had become one.

"Don't you want a normal relationship?"

His sister was pushing it. "What's normal to you isn't necessarily normal to me."

"Apparently."

He gave her a look. "The only one here that has a problem with it is you."

"I just don't get it… Why do you need to be with two people? One of them being a man."

"You don't have to, Gayle. You don't have to understand my relationship with Paige and Connor."

She sighed, the frustration clear.

"Why don't you go swimming?" he suggested, trying to change the subject.

Gayle gaped at him in horror. "Do you know how much I paid for this hair?"

"Fine. Don't go swimming."

Paige screamed when Connor picked her up and threw her into the deep end. He dove in quickly after her and came up laughing. Paige surfaced, sputtering and cursing at him.

Even Gryff laughed loudly.

Paige pretended to be angry, and Connor yelled, "Aw, baby. You know I love you!"

"Do they call you that? Do they tell you that?"

Anger bubbled up enough for him to snap, "Gayle, give it a rest."

"I love you, big brother. I don't want to see you get hurt again."

"I'll be fine."

"I hope so."

Grae hoped so too.

CHAPTER 10

Grae stood at the kitchen sink and gazed out of the window onto the back patio. Connor sat in one of those green plastic Adirondack chairs with Paige in his lap. Their foreheads were pinned together, and their laughter surrounded them.

A sharp twinge had him grimacing. He rubbed at his chest in an attempt to relieve the pain.

Grae had been watching Connor play with Paige's fingers for the last few minutes. Kissing them, intertwining his with hers, comparing hand sizes, and spinning her wedding ring.

It was the ring that bothered Grae the most since it symbolized the two of them belonging to each other for infinity. But if he were honest with himself, it was the whole scene before him causing the ache. He wasn't one to fear much, but watching the two of them together scared him. It brought back the memories of his last failed threesome.

Grae was the one who had suggested the idea to his then live-in girlfriend. At first, she was reluctant, but after meeting Joshua, she had quickly agreed. Maybe that should have given him a clue. It worked out well...until it didn't. No rules had been established, leaving the relationship more organic. Grae had remained in his home with his girlfriend, while Joshua continued to live in his own condo. But they got together often.

Then suddenly, Grae's bed was more empty than not.

When he least expected it, he became the third wheel. The afterthought.

One day, he came home to an empty house. Her closets had been emptied, her personal belongings gone. His girlfriend of three years had moved out and into Joshua's place.

He couldn't go through that again.

He couldn't let it get that far. He couldn't let himself show that type of weakness again.

Ever.

Now his greatest fear was that it was happening. He was becoming vulnerable and setting himself up for a whole lot of hurt.

He went into this relationship knowing he was already at a disadvantage. But he had such an instant attraction to Paige, he thought it would be worth the risk.

Looking at them now, he realized how wrong he might be.

Not only was he still living in their house, Paige and Connor continued to function mainly as a couple, instead of a threesome. He wasn't sure if they were even aware of it.

From the beginning, he'd been envious of their intimacy, their partnership, and had wanted to become a part of it. *Needed* to become a part of it for the relationship to succeed. But even after months, it wasn't quite where it should be. At least in Grae's view.

Plus, he wasn't the most patient man.

Nothing made the division more clear than the other night when Connor came home and said he was invited to dinner with the owner of his engineering firm. So, of course, he was taking his wife. Because of their unconventional relationship, it shouldn't have bothered him, but it did. And Grae did not like that feeling.

It had been three months since he'd moved into their house, a change that was supposed to be temporary, but Grae still didn't think the time was right to broach the subject of permanency. With moving them into his house. Or with their relationship.

Now, looking at his two lovers cozying up together outside, he figured he was right in waiting.

Three months had been more than enough time for them to gel as a threesome. To be something more than just sex.

When Grae was younger, he never thought he would ever want to settle down. He had the world by the balls. He was young, healthy, in shape, and had a very lucrative career in front of him. Now, being older, he thought about nothing but settling down. Even if it would be in an unusual relationship.

So, if it wasn't going to happen…if the relationship was going to fail, now would be the time to walk away. Before it got any harder.

Grae closed his eyes, his hands clutching the edge of the sink.

The problem was he allowed himself to get attached to them. To feel something. Was the feeling as strong as what Paige and Connor had for each other? He wasn't sure. Did they even have any type of feelings for him?

Yes, they cared about him. Yes, they wanted him in their bed…

He let out an explosive curse.

"Are you okay?"

Grae cursed again, but this time, he did it under his breath.

"Are you in pain?" Paige looked concerned.

Not the pain you're thinking of, Grae thought. "I'm fine."

She stopped inches in front of him, hands on hips, and searched his face. "Don't give me that bullshit. Is it your heart?" she asked.

Grae wanted to laugh. If she only knew. He shook his head. "No."

"What is it then?"

Grae hesitated and regarded the woman in front of him. He didn't realize how strong his feelings were for her until that precise moment. His attraction and uncontrollable possessiveness of her had transformed in the past few months.

Did he want this woman for himself? *Hell, yes.*

Would it be easier if Connor were out of the picture? Of course. But Paige made it quite clear in the beginning they were a package deal, and he had accepted that. Anyway, he would never try to steal away someone's wife. Share her, yes. Steal her, no.

His gaze raked Paige from her long, dark hair hanging loosely around her shoulders, over her nipples which were discernable through her tight tank top, over the curve of her hips encased in khaki shorts, and down her legs, all the way to the polished toes of her bare feet.

His heart squeezed again, making him take a long, calming breath.

He didn't know if he could walk away from this woman. But he didn't know if he could live with how things were either. "Is me being here just an excuse for you to have an affair, Paige? Or am I only here for Connor's exploration?" He knew the answers to his questions, and he regretted them as soon as he asked them. But he wanted someone else to share the pain he felt right now. Fair or not. It was petty, but at the moment, he wasn't feeling magnanimous.

Her eyebrows shot to her hairline, confusion crossing her face. "What the hell are you talking about, Grae?"

"Am I just a temporary thrill? I see you two out there…" He stopped. He sounded like a scorned lover and he didn't feel proud that he'd let himself stoop so low. To let his doubts control him.

Paige's gaze flicked out the window to where Grae could only assume Connor still waited for his wife. "I don't understand…" she trailed off.

Yes, he believed her. He knew she was confused and not sure where he was coming from. He knew it because he felt confused himself. "I'm aware that I've come into this relationship late. But I was hoping it would smooth out sooner than later. If I weren't here, you two would still do what you do... have sex, date, have a complete life. Why am I here? Why do you even need me involved?"

Paige stared at the man in front of her like she'd never seen him before. Because she hadn't. Emotions were overtaking him and in the three months that they'd lived together, slept together, ate together—besides the anger of her going behind his back to watch the game tape where he collapsed—she'd never seen this type of reaction from him.

It not only caught her off guard, but it scared her. Had he been bottling this up?

And why now?

Paige's gaze went back out to Connor, waiting for her to bring him a beer. Had Grae been watching them?

She thought about what the two of them had been doing out there. Not only enjoying the beautiful day but each other. Then that's what couples in love did, right?

Fuck.

It dawned on her about how she was thinking. She and Connor *were* the problem. They still acted as a couple. Probably causing Grae to feel left out when they hadn't meant to.

"You call each other honey and baby. We have no pet names for each other."

Once again, his words surprised her. "I didn't realize you would want a pet name. You don't seem the type. You're not the kind of man I'd call snookums." She was being facetious, but honest. "What do you want me to call you?" she asked carefully.

"If you have to ask..."

Paige rolled her eyes and stepped away from him, her anger flaring. "I never thought you'd be one to play emotional blackmail,

Grae. Never. I can't imagine what's sparking this now, except for jealousy. Is that what it is?"

Grae's expression remained blank, his eyes not wavering, nothing in his body moving except for a tick in his jaw.

"Are you jealous of me? Or of Connor?" she asked him. Her gaze raked his face for any little sign.

"I'm jealous of what the two of you have. I didn't think I was, but I am. And jealousy, even doubts, don't work in this type of relationship." He shook his head. "They just don't."

Paige slapped her palm against her chest. "*I* know that. I know that because I'm surrounded by polyamorous relationships. But, tell me… How do *you* know that?"

Other than common sense, of course. But now it was time to find out the truth. To find out what Gayle hinted at and what Paige suspected. She was tired of him holding back. She jammed a finger into his chest. "How? Tell me what happened when you tried this before."

"I never said I've done this before." His nostrils flared, and his mouth became an angry slash.

His avoidance of his past pissed her off even more. "Don't lie to me. I can feel it in here." She pointed to her own heart this time. "And your sister let it slip!" Graedon didn't respond, making her even more frustrated. "Why won't you talk about it?" she practically shouted at him.

His face darkened. "Because I don't need to. It's not us!"

Paige was surprised when he raised his voice. He normally kept his composure, no matter what happened. But this was affecting him much more than she realized.

He grabbed her hands and lifted them to his lips. "That's not us," he said more softly. "I don't want it to be."

"Help us make this work, Grae." She sounded desperate, begging—and she was. Because what she saw so far in this kitchen wasn't a good sign for their relationship. Paige did not want this to go south. She swallowed hard, willing her panic to subside.

"Paige…" he whispered.

"No." She shook her head. "Tell us what we need to do to make this work between all of us. *Please.*"

He closed his eyes and nodded. When he opened them, they were filled with pain and sadness.

This was *so* not the Graedon she knew. No. This was a peek at someone different. An old piece of himself, maybe.

"Paige, I want you and Connor in my life. But…"

"But?" Her heart stopped, and she held her breath.

"But you were an established couple. A married couple. You had…have an existing relationship. It feels like you cracked that open just to wedge me in. We need to be a whole. A unit. Not you two as an entrée with me as a side dish."

If his expression weren't so serious, she would've laughed at his analogy. But what was happening wasn't funny. Not at all. It was breaking her heart. "I'm sorry." Her eyes burned, but she wasn't going to cry, damn it! "I'm sorry if you've ever felt that way."

"It's hard not to when the two people you love already loved each other, knew each other inside and out, knew each other's habits and pet peeves."

Jesus, he just admitted he *loved* them, so why was this such a problem? People who loved each other should be able to iron out any wrinkle that came along. "But you knew that was an obstacle to overcome when we began."

"You're right. I did," he said, solemnly. "I also didn't expect to fall in love with you so quickly. To bond so deeply with Connor. I think that was my hiccup." He released a loud breath.

Paige fought not to scream her next words. "That's not a hiccup! I hate hiccups!"

"Did you say you love us?" Connor's voice came from the doorway to the patio.

Grae hesitated for a moment, regarding Connor. "I did."

Connor stepped closer, wearing a frown. "And are you thinking about leaving?"

Paige's panic rose again. "Grae, you *cannot* leave! Holy shit!" She spun away and moved to the other side of the kitchen, her heart now pounding furiously, her body beginning to shake.

No. No. No.

Grae could not leave. Especially after he just said he loved them. Not just her, which she suspected, but Connor too. She didn't know if it just slipped out or he had planned to tell them. Although, she strongly suspected it wasn't planned since that emotional bond hadn't been discussed between the three of them. Paige closed her eyes. She realized now, she and Connor said it to each other all the time. Even in front of Grae.

Fuck.

She couldn't imagine being in a triad where only two of the three people told each other that they loved each other on a regular basis. In the beginning, it'd been different. She knew it was attraction and lust binding them together. But now...

In the last three months, it became way more than that. And she couldn't pinpoint when.

She wondered how Connor felt about Grae, but she hesitated to ask him in front of the other man. Especially since Grae was at a tipping point. If Connor faltered with his answer for even a second...

"Maybe I just need to step back for a bit. Let you two decide if this is something you really want. If you can love me as much as you love each other."

Paige shook her head, biting her bottom lip. Neither she nor Connor had ever indicated that this was something they *didn't* want. They had never said they didn't love him.

But they've never told him they did, either.

Fuck. And here she thought everything had been going smoothly.

"Look. I need to go on the road anyway. There are some

summer college football camps I want to attend to scout some players."

Paige wondered if he was simply looking for an excuse to take a break. He didn't have to go. He could send one of his people to do that.

"If that's what you need to do…" Connor said, leaning against the counter, studying Grae.

Paige shot him a deadly glare. He shouldn't be encouraging Grae to leave, even it ended up being temporary.

"Paige, don't give me that look. If Grae needs to go, he needs to go. He needs to do what's best for him." Connor looked at Grae. "Just know that we don't want you to leave. But we respect your decision, and we'll be here when you get back."

Grae's expression relaxed a bit.

Paige wanted to drop to her knees and desperately beg for him not to go. Maybe Connor was right; Grae needed space. She tried to collect her racing thoughts. "How long are you going to be gone?"

"I figure a month. I'm going to hit as many camps as I can."

"When are you leaving?" Connor asked quietly.

Paige realized he wasn't happy about all this either.

"Tonight. I'm going to head home, pack, and hit the road."

"Wait. Did you have this planned?" Paige asked, her head spinning. How long had he known he was going away?

"No. But it's something I need to do."

Those words hit Paige hard, and she realized they had a double meaning. She nodded and accepted the inevitable. She tried to console herself with the fact that it would only be a month.

Hopefully.

CHAPTER 11

Y*ou need to come home.* Paige pushed Send on her cell phone.

She felt lonely and missed Grae so much her heart hurt. The ache in her chest couldn't get any worse.

It had only been two weeks since he'd been on the road in his hunt for talent. Or, what Paige supposed was to get "clarification" on their relationship.

Whichever was the real reason, Paige knew what she wanted. Connor also knew what he wanted. They'd talked about it every night until they were both exhausted from discussing it.

It was bad enough Grae left, but he wasn't communicating with them either. He'd cut off all dialogue. Leaving was the cut of the knife, silence—the twist of the blade.

Connor became quiet, sad. So unlike himself. Even so, he told her to leave it alone. Let Grae have his space.

Paige had a hard time doing this. She'd even been tempted to call Grae's sister, Gayle, to find out what really happened in his last relationship.

Grae would probably never forgive her for sticking her nose where it didn't belong.

And she wouldn't blame him.

As the minutes ticked by, Paige paced, constantly looking at her phone, willing the damn thing to make a noise indicating an incoming text.

After a few more minutes, she sighed and reluctantly put the phone on the coffee table, turning on the TV. She needed to get her mind off Grae. She laughed at herself. Like that was going to happen.

She settled on the couch and flipped through the channels, too restless to find anything she could concentrate on. She chewed on her bottom lip. A typical Grae reprimand popped into her head and she stopped. She used to appreciate an empty house, time to herself. Now, not so much. Both the house and she felt hollow, empty.

Did Grae even miss them at all?

She started when her phone dinged and scrambled to grab it, looking at the screen.

Why? Because Connor is gone?

How did he even know Connor was on another business trip? Were they talking?

She felt tempted to call Connor to ask him, but since she had Grae's attention, she needed to try to convince him what he meant to them, why this was important to her and Connor. Prove to him their relationship was more than just sex, physical pleasure, and release.

Grae's leaving had left them with a missing piece in their relationship, something Paige never thought could happen to their tight marriage. A hole that surprised both her and Connor.

Until he left, she didn't think either Connor or she realized how important he was to them.

How selfish they'd been.

How stupid they'd been by constantly telling each other that they loved each other but not including Grae in on the sentiment.

She blew out a breath and typed a text. *No. Because we miss you. You're a part of us.*

Paige stared at the screen and willed him to respond. The seconds seemed like minutes, the minutes like hours, as she waited for an incoming text. She flopped on the couch, laying on her stomach, and tucked her head into crossed arms. She wanted to scream, kick her legs, have a temper tantrum. Instead, she worked on slowing her breathing in an attempt to control her anxiety. She desperately wished Connor was here.

Hell. *Both* of her men were too far away. She needed them now. She needed to touch them.

Her heart cracked a little more when the phone's screen remained dark.

She typed another text, then stared at it. Her finger hesitated over the Send button. She swallowed hard and finally sent it on its way.

Because we love you.

It wasn't the way she wanted to tell him, in an impersonal text. She'd wanted to tell him in person. But if her admitting it to him now would make him consider coming home, then she needed to jump on the opportunity. Not later and risk losing him forever.

Paige dropped her head back down and sighed, her eyes burning enough that she rubbed them.

Maybe she should have just left it alone like Connor had said. Let Grae come home when he felt ready.

She was fucking stupid for pushing him.

"Do you?"

Paige gasped and leaped off the couch.

Grae leaned against the entrance to the living room. His face looked solemn and serious.

She didn't know if she should run up to him to hug him and hold him tight because he was home to stay. Or if he was here to pack what was left of his stuff in the house.

He pushed off the wall.

Now Paige noticed the suitcase in the hall. She hoped it was the one he'd taken on his trip. And not one he came to fill. "Is that suitcase empty or full?" she asked, cautiously.

"Full."

She released a breath, desperately wanting to believe that was a good sign.

"Answer my question, Paige." He stepped over to her, almost toe to toe, looking down, searching her face.

"Yes, Grae. We love you. We're here for you. We want you to be a part of our lives. Whether you believe it or not, that was never a question for us. But we need you to *want* to be here. We want you to be happy." A rogue tear escaped, and she wiped it away quickly. "I'm sorry if you've ever felt excluded." She placed her hands on his chest, and his heartbeat was rapid and strong beneath her palm.

With a quickness she wasn't expecting, he snagged her wrists and pulled her to him tight. He pressed his lips to the top of her head. "You belong to me, Paige." His voice sounded low, muffled in her hair. "So does Connor."

"Yes," she hissed softly. She wrapped her arms around his waist, squeezing him and never wanting to let him go.

"We belong to each other," he continued. "It's the only way this will ever work."

"Yes. The three of us belong to each other," she repeated. She tilted her face up to him.

Grae lowered his head until his lips were just a breath away. "God, I can't believe how much I love you," he murmured.

She would address why he couldn't believe it later because right now she just felt happy that he did. "We need to call Connor."

"No, we don't," he said.

She stared at him curiously.

He glanced at his watch. "He'll be here soon. I called him and told him to cut his trip short and get home as soon as possible."

She gave him a relieved smile and looked up into his dark eyes. "Kiss me," she breathed.

Then he did.

Grae crushed his lips against hers, parting them with her tongue to explore her mouth. Their tongues tangled and he deepened the kiss until she was breathless. Her body hummed with wanting him, needing to feel his warm skin against hers.

"Can I join in?" Connor asked from the hallway. His voice held a little bit of excitement and also some relief.

Grae stepped back to open up their embrace and held out a hand to Connor. "Absolutely."

With a wide smile, Connor crushed the three of them together in an awkward hug. They took turns kissing each other and laughing because it was the dorkiest thing ever, at least to Paige anyway.

Then the laughter turned to sighs and moans as things got serious. Two weeks had been too long without Grae in their bed.

They pulled at each other's clothes until the living room was littered. They licked, kissed, nipped, touched, stroked, and plucked until they fell into a heap on the floor.

Grae's cock was heavy with need, pressing against Paige's thigh. Connor's erection was as hard as steel sliding along her belly. She wanted one of them inside her, and she didn't care who.

No, she didn't want one of them, she wanted *both*. Her realization made her pussy clench, becoming slick.

She pulled her mouth away from Connor's chest. "I want you both."

"We want you too." Connor groaned as Grae stroked his length.

"No. *Both*."

Grae lifted his head. "Like the fantasy you told me?"

"Yes. We haven't done it yet."

"What are we waiting for?" Connor asked. "You want us to tie you up too?"

"Yes. Spank me, fuck me, tie me up. I want it all."

"*Jesus,*" Connor whispered, looking at Grae as if checking to see if he heard the same thing.

Grae gave him a little nod.

"Here or in the bedroom?"

"In the bedroom," Grae answered. "I have an idea."

The words *I have an idea* sent lightning through Paige's core.

Holy shit, this was really going to happen!

Grae stood, pulled Paige into his arms, and picked her up like she was as light as a feather. He looked at Connor, who still laid on the floor, with impatience. "Let's go."

Connor chuckled at the roughness of Grae's command. "Don't worry. There is no way in hell that I'm missing out on this."

They went into the bedroom and Grae placed her on her feet. He told Connor to get the condoms and lube out of the drawer, while Grae dug through Connor's closet for ties.

"Oh, no. Not that one. It's my favorite," Connor said as Grae pulled a couple out of the closet.

Grae hung it back up and grabbed another, showing them to Connor for approval.

Connor nodded. Holding a strip of condoms and a bottle of Astroglide, he came to the end of the bed, where Paige stood. He threw the items onto the mattress and stepped behind her. Wrapping his arms around her waist, he licked along the back of her neck, nuzzling her hair to the side. Then he laid kisses along her spine, making her shiver, hardening her nipples to points.

Grae stepped in front of her, three neckties in his hands.

Paige stared at them with nervous excitement, wondering why he needed three. She was sure she would find out before long. She took in the size of Grae's erection. "Uh, maybe we should first figure out who is going where."

Grae slid one necktie around her throat, tightening it slightly. "Don't worry about that. We'll figure it out."

The narrow fabric of Connor's tie closed in around her neck

until it was snug. Paige didn't panic because it was Grae. She trusted him. He would never do anything to hurt her.

He let the one end go, and the silky fabric slid along her skin, giving her goosebumps.

He handed one of the ties to Connor. "Tie her arms behind her."

"We're not tying her to the bed?" he asked, surprised.

"No. Not for what I have planned."

Paige's knees buckled, and Grae caught her, holding her weight up while Connor took her wrists then placed them at the small of her back, wrapping the fabric around, binding her hands together.

When he released her, she tested the knot, and it held. Her breath became shallow, and she began to tremble, keeping her gaze locked on Grae. He brushed the next tie over her parted lips and for a moment, she thought he would gag her.

But he swept it along her cheek, one side then the other. Then down, moving the silk over her puckered nipples and between her breasts, teasing her. He traced the tip of it down her belly and brushed it between her legs along her crease.

Paige bit her bottom lip.

Grae quickly noticed. "You do want to be spanked, don't you?" His eyes were dark and hooded as his erection twitched.

She assumed it was from the thought of him slapping his palm against her ass. "*Yes.*"

He handed the second tie to Connor. "Blindfold her."

Connor did as he was told, the bedroom and her men disappearing as he tightened the fabric over her eyes. Her breathing shallowed.

She'd never, ever been blindfolded before.

Now she was forced to use her other senses to figure out what they were doing. Her nostrils flared to take in their scents. Her hearing became attuned to every minor movement of their bodies, their breathing. Until her eyes were covered, she didn't even realize how heavy Connor was breathing or the raggedness of Grae's.

She waited for Connor or Grae to ask her if she felt sure she wanted this. But they didn't. Most likely, they didn't want her to have second thoughts.

Grae slithered the remaining tie around her waist like a snake, down her thighs, around her knees, in between her ankles.

There was no way he was going to hobble her. That would make it difficult for them to fuck her. Especially both of them. At the same time.

Her body quaked at the image of them both being inside her. She gasped and squeezed her eyes tighter underneath the makeshift blindfold. Paige could feel the movement of air against her heated skin as Grae stood.

"Gag her."

Cloth slid into her mouth, against her tongue, between her teeth. She felt like a horse with a bit in its mouth. She guessed it was fitting since they were about to ride her.

Suddenly they were gone. The air around her empty as she stood bound, blind, and mute at the end of the bed.

Arousal dampened her inner thighs as she waited.

Then she heard the sound of kissing and groaning. And she cursed the blindfold. She couldn't see her men's mouths on each other, the explorations of their tongues. Their hard lengths pressing against each other.

The gag kept her from complaining.

Grae murmured something to Connor.

Paige strained to hear what it was. Damn it, she couldn't even demand that he tell her. She was under their complete control by being helpless. She screamed around the gag.

The response she got was a chuckle out of Grae. "Ah. Someone is getting impatient."

Getting? She was already there.

"Connor, sit on the edge of the bed."

Paige could feel them moving around her. One of them grabbed her—Grae, she thought—and positioned her facing the bed. Then she felt Connor's thighs on each side of hers. His hands cupped her breasts, and his lips captured a nipple, sucking it deep into his mouth, his fingers tugging and twisting the other one.

Grae's erection pressed into the crease of her ass momentarily as he kissed along her back, his hands smoothing along her ribs, waist, and then hips. He reached between her thighs, testing her wetness and made a sound of approval. His long fingers traced along the edges of her swollen lips, finding her clit—so sensitive to his touch.

She jerked as he circled it, the pressure hard and relentless. Her gasp muffled by the necktie as he plunged two fingers inside her.

"She's so ready for you to take her," he told Connor.

She clamped down on his fingers as he worked them in and out.

Connor dropped to his knees at her feet and, within seconds, he had his mouth on her, sucking her clit, flicking her with his tongue.

Ah fuck. She was going to come, and she couldn't tell them not to stop until she did. She couldn't encourage Grae to fuck her harder and faster with his fingers. The tension at her center kept building, and her thighs began to tremble. She slammed her head back against Grae's chest. His arm wrapped around the front of her shoulders, holding her tight against him as he and Connor worked their magic.

Her hands were pinned behind her, between their bodies. She wiggled her fingers trying to reach him, trying to find his cock. But he was just out of reach. She screamed again in frustration, and the scream turned into a groan as an orgasm rippled through her. Connor grabbed her behind the thighs and Grae tightened his hold on her to keep her from collapsing. When the last waves of climax waned, Grae slipped his fingers from her and Connor moved away.

"Sit back on the bed." Grae's voice sounded rough, low and close to her ear.

The bed groaned when Connor settled back into position.

With hands on her hips, Grae moved her forward. "Grab her arms to help her."

"Baby, climb up on my lap," Connor coaxed her, with a grip on her elbows. As she settled on his lap, he groaned, "That's it. Fuck, I can feel how wet you are." She straddled him, the length of his cock pressing against her opening. Connor grabbed a handful of her ass. "Lift up."

She rose, then sank onto him until his cock was deep within her. All the breath rushed out of her around the gag. She lifted and lowered herself, ready to come again. She didn't want to wait. She couldn't wait.

Connor cursed, grabbing her waist since Grae still had a firm grip on her hips. "Baby, you have to wait. You have to go slow. *Fuck*."

Grae's moved his hands up to her breasts and pinched both of her nipples hard, then twisted them between his forefingers and thumbs.

All this did was make her grind even harder against Connor. He cursed again.

"Lay back," Grae ordered.

Connor fell back onto the mattress, bringing Paige with him.

Grae moved up tight against her, between Connor's thighs.

The tear of the condom wrapper seemed loud in the room, even with their rapid, ragged breathing. The snap of the cap on the lube brought home the reality that this really was going to happen. Her fantasy was really going to—

The sting of Grae's hand against her ass made her jerk, almost unseating her from Connor.

Fuck!

Paige felt the cool air before feeling the sharp smack of his hand against her other cheek.

Oh fuck.

"Every time you smack her she clenches around me so tight. It's fucking amazing," Connor said from between what sounded like gritted teeth.

"Her ass is so red," Grae said.

Whether he spoke to Connor or himself, she didn't know. Paige tensed, waiting for the next swat.

Instead, he smoothed a hand over her angry skin, kissing each cheek gently.

She moaned into the fabric and relaxed her muscles. The coolness of the lube dripping between her ass cheeks made her squirm, which made Connor groan and hold her still.

Grae's thumb found her anus and worked the lube around. He squirted more lube and pressed his thumb just inside her tight ring. "Your ass is so tight," he murmured, pressing his thumb into her slightly until it slipped in and out of her easily. He slid his thumb out and replaced it with two of his long fingers. More lube, more pressure.

She willed herself to stay relaxed at the strange feeling of fullness back there.

"Grae, *fuck...*" Connor groaned. "We gotta do this before I come."

Grae didn't respond. Instead, he smacked Paige's ass again.

She squealed, not expecting it—then he was inside her. Not fully. Because that seemed impossible. It would have been difficult even if Connor wasn't inside her also. The pressure was immense, and she squeezed her eyes shut, concentrating on what he was doing.

He moved slowly, pressing, pushing, making her stretch. His fingers trembled where they gripped her hips. His breath came out in spurts.

Connor's fingers pressed her clit, circling it, making her open wider to accept both of them.

Holy fuck, she had both of her men inside her at the same time.

"You need to start moving, Connor. Opposite me."

What?

Luckily, Connor knew what Grae meant, and he moved in and out of her slowly. As Connor entered her, Grae pulled back. As Grae entered her, seating himself even deeper this time, Connor pulled out almost completely. Each move they made created room for the other. Until they were taking turns being balls deep within her.

Paige was losing her mind. This absolutely was the most incredible feeling of fullness she'd ever experience. They were going slow and being careful, but the snail's pace drove her to the edge even sooner. Her body accepted both of them, and just this thought made her come…hard.

She cried out, wanting to grip something during the strong pulsations of her orgasm, but she couldn't. Her hands were still bound behind her back.

Both hesitated during her climax; she heard a hiss from Connor and a sound deep from the back of Grae's throat. She could only imagine both of them were hanging by a thread.

Grae smacked her again, harder this time.

Paige slammed her hips down onto Connor, determined to quicken the pace.

"Fuck, baby. Fuck, baby," Connor began to repeat, mindlessly. "Oh fuck!" His thumb rubbed her clit at a frenzied pace, causing her to clench down on him harder.

Doing this must've made Grae's entry more difficult. "Are you going to come again, Paige?" Grae asked her.

She nodded her head.

"Connor?"

"Oh, fuck yes. I'm ready," he grunted.

"Paige, you're going to come when I tell you. Understand?"

Paige nodded again. Fuck, if he could make her come on command, she was never letting him leave the house again.

Grae pushed even deeper inside her.

She hadn't realized he wasn't fully seated. The stretch caused an almost painful pleasure run through her. Then she was quickly back at the beginning of an orgasm. Her heart pounded, her breath caught, and when Grae entered her again, he told her to come.

She could do nothing but.

Connor cursed as he released deep inside her and Grae grunted, his fingers digging into her flesh.

Paige collapsed all her weight onto Connor's heaving chest, resting her cheek on his damp skin. He ripped the blindfold off her head and untied her gag, throwing the neckties to the side.

Grae released her wrists before pulling out of her and heading to the bathroom.

Paige rubbed the circulation back into her hands as she slid her gaze to her husband's face.

He looked quite content. And spent. His eyes were unfocused, his breathing still uneven—he wore a Cheshire cat smile. He brushed the hair out of her face, off of her damp skin. "Damn. Was it everything you expected in a tie-me-up-spank-me-double-team fantasy?"

"Hell, yes."

"Good," Grae said as he returned. His weight dipped the mattress as he settled onto his side of the bed. He looked relaxed and spent also.

Paige felt sure she looked the same. She needed a shower. First, she needed to know one thing... "Were you two talking behind my back?"

The men glanced at each other, smiled, and then back at her.

"We're going to have a discussion about that when I get out of the shower." She only pretended to bust their balls, because whatever happened, whatever had been said, whatever Connor did to help Grae come home, she didn't care. She just felt glad he was here. She also felt ready to make sure she and Connor did better at including Grae as a partner in the future.

And for the rest of their lives.

EPILOGUE

Paige sat sideways in Grae's lap using his arm and part of his broad chest as her backrest. Her legs laid across Connor's lap as he sat in the lounge chair next to them. His head was back and his eyes closed, her husband smoothing his palms mindlessly back and forth over her calves.

Logan's German shepherd, Magnum, sat at Ty's feet as the man tended to the New York strips on the grill. The dog's tongue hung out. Paige could swear a string of drool clung from it. Not that she blamed the dog. With the number of steaks, there had to be half of a cow on that grill. Her own mouth watered just thinking about it.

Logan fished a beer out of a huge tub of ice sitting in the corner of the enormous deck. He tossed one to Connor, who caught it with ease. So much for thinking Connor was drifting off to sleep on this warm Labor Day Monday.

"Should have been a receiver, Con," Logan said, grinning.

Paige shot her brother an exaggerated scowl. The last thing they needed was to get Connor on the subject of football so she would have to hear about the differences between Australian and

American football for the millionth time. Especially today when Connor was outnumbered by former NFL football players.

Quinn came out of the house, her belly leading the way. It was bigger with this pregnancy than the last. One hand held her distended stomach as she tried to carry a huge bowl of macaroni salad with the other.

"You got that?" Paige asked, ready to jump up and help.

Quinn waved a hand at her, indicating for her to stay where she was. She wedged the bowl against the curve of her belly to keep from dropping it.

Paige knew if she did all the big tough football players would cry. Quinn's mac salad was bangin'.

"I'm fine. You look comfy all sprawled out over your men."

My men.

Yes, they were.

"And anyway," she continued, while she waddled over to the large table set up under the shade. "The guys are right behind me, bringing the rest of the food." She got a dreamy look on her face. "Wait until you taste Eve's peach cobbler. It's to die for."

Ren Landis stepped through the open doorway, carrying a large tray full of food. "Yeah, she'd know. I had to keep smacking her fingers, or there would be none for the rest of us."

"Ooo. You chased a pregnant woman away from food?" Paige asked him. "And you didn't get kicked in the nuts?"

Ren laughed. "I saw my life flash before my eyes, but I figured saving the cobbler was worth the sacrifice." He put the tray down on the table and then relieved Quinn of the revered macaroni salad. Slipping behind Quinn, he wrapped his arms around her extended waist and rubbed her belly.

Quinn smiled and patted his hands.

Paige couldn't help but notice her brother stiffen and take a step forward.

"You've got a death wish," Ty said to his friend, chuckling, as he turned back to flip the steaks.

Ren gave Logan a wide grin while giving Quinn a big peck on the cheek and then backed away, his hands up in surrender.

"One day I'm just going to kick your ass," Logan said. Unfortunately, he wasn't joking.

"You can try," Ren answered.

The testosterone level on the deck rose a few notches, and Paige wondered if they were going to have to break up an actual fight. Ren always knew how to push Logan's buttons. And he enjoyed doing it.

But as soon as Cole Dixon came outside carrying Preston, the men dropped their unspoken challenge to focus on the toddler in Cole's arms. Especially when Cole said, "I think someone took a shit in his diaper."

"Jeez, Cole, nice mouth around my kid," Logan said, frowning. "And it's a pull-up, not a diaper."

"Don't you need the practice, Cole?" Quinn called out from a seat in the shade, laughing.

"Ah, nope."

"Oh yes, he does," Eve said as she walked up the steps to the deck from the yard. She'd taken a little of what Connor called a walk-about. Her own baby bump was half the size of Quinn's but still very noticeable. She'd taken a stroll in an attempt to loosen the tight muscles in her back.

"That shit better not be contagious," Paige muttered. She felt Grae's body shake before she heard the chuckle. "Not funny, Grae. I'm serious."

"I would love to see your belly fat with our child."

Fat. Child.

No.

She shivered at his words, picturing herself carrying his or Connor's child inside of her. She fought back the unwanted sentiment. "Fuck you."

"Big ears!" Logan yelled, tilting his head toward Preston.

"That mouth," Grae admonished, shaking his head.

Paige frowned. She reminded herself that pregnancy looked and probably felt miserable and painful. "We'll get a dog," she compromised.

Connor patted her leg as Grae laughed.

Grae almost dumped Paige's ass onto the deck as he stood. "I'll change him. I could use the practice," he said *very* loudly.

All eyes turned to Paige.

Now, real heat crept up her cheeks. "I am *not* pregnant. Holy hell."

Grae laughed as he took Preston out of Cole's arms and into the house.

"Does he know what he's doing?" Quinn asked in a loud stage whisper from across the deck.

"How the hell do I know?" Paige answered.

They were all looking at her like she should go in and help him.

Well, she was not going to do it. He volunteered, so tough shit. Literally. "It's a damn pull-up, not rocket science."

Logan shook his head and settled next to Quinn, keeping an eye on Ren.

Of course, Ren just ate that up.

Paige wondered when her brother would realize the man wasn't trying to steal Logan's wife. Ren had his hands full with Cole and Eve. And soon with their own child.

"When are you due?" Connor asked Quinn.

"Not soon enough," Quinn said.

"How many kids do you three plan on having?" Eve asked.

"As many as it takes until one comes out chocolate," Ty said, loading the perfectly grilled steaks on a platter and carrying them over to the table.

"Then this one better come out chocolate with dark chocolate chunks, Ty. Because I want my body back," Quinn told her husband.

"Oh God," Eve cried, placing a hand on her belly. "Is that what

I have to look forward to?" She looked back and forth between Cole and Ren with a panicked expression.

"Baby, we're both chocolate. One milk, one dark. So, it's all good," Ren said, leaning over to rub her stomach.

Paige wanted to point out that Cole wasn't even dark enough to be considered milk chocolate. Vanilla chocolate, maybe. But now was probably not the time and she was smart enough to keep her mouth shut.

Grae came back out with Preston wearing a fresh pull-up. The mission was a success.

Paige had to admit, seeing Preston's little toddler hand in Grae's massive one as the child tottered out onto the deck made her heart melt a little. Grae would make a good father. Strict, but good. She looked over at her husband. Connor would be the good cop to their kids, Grae the bad cop.

Paige shook her head. What was she thinking?

Grrr.

She needed to remember to refill her birth control.

"All right, let's eat," Logan called out.

Grae handed Preston over to his father, who settled the little one into a high chair between him and Ty.

Their smooth co-parenting as fathers always amazed Paige. "You know, seeing all these threesomes makes me realize we're a weird bunch," Paige said out loud.

"Meh. Maybe we'll become the new normal," Eve said, stuffing her face with the scrumptious mac salad.

"This isn't Utah," Cole stated, taking a bite into a warm, buttered dinner roll.

Paige giggled. No, it wasn't. But who cared? Love was love. Right?

With baby Preston at the table, there was ten of them. A crazy extended family of sorts. And soon there would be a dozen.

"I'm glad you guys got over your little rough patch this

summer," Logan said solemnly, looking between Connor, Grae, and his sister.

Paige tensed since she knew Grae hated his personal business being out there.

"Those two weeks were the toughest I've dealt with since my heart surgery. That time away really showed me how much I can't live without either of them."

His words totally floored her. *Who is this man?* Paige turned her head to stare at him open mouthed.

"Close your mouth," Grae told her softly.

"Same here," Connor said. "Believe me, the thought that he might not return scared us."

"Being open and painfully honest is the only way this sh—" Cole came to a screeching halt, staring at Preston. "Stuff works."

Eve gave him a smile and reached under the table to pat his thigh.

"Are you glad to finally be back in your house, Grae?" Ty asked.

Paige wouldn't be surprised if Grae jumped out of his chair, ran around the deck like a madman, and screamed, "Yes, yes, yes!" at the top of his lungs.

He would never do that, but still...

"At least, our house has a pool," Connor said. He was getting used to saying *our house* instead of *Grae's house*. They both were. "You guys have a huge yard, you need a pool."

Logan gave him a look. "Unless you want to pay for it, swim in your own. Kids are expensive."

"They sure are. I can't wait for Preston to be old enough to drive a tractor, we'll put him to work mowing the sod fields. He needs to earn his keep," Ty said, smirking.

"You've got a few years to go until that, honey," Quinn interjected around a mouthful of peach cobbler. She was starting with dessert first. Well, nobody had a death wish to tell the pregnant woman otherwise.

"We've decided to get him a toy tractor for Christmas," Logan said.

"And a pair of work gloves," Ty added, jokingly.

After they had eaten, they spread out around the deck, enjoying the great early September weather. Preston was off taking a nap. The men flanked their women, drinking beer and joking with each other.

Everyone here was truly happy. A feeling of contentment overcame Paige as she sat watching the group.

Ty and Quinn were the best things to ever happen to Logan. Ren and Cole were the best things to ever happen to Eve.

Then as Paige looked over at Grae, she realized he was the best thing to happen to her and her husband. The past couple months since they've moved out of their house and into Grae's had cemented their relationship. They were now living as a unit. Their marriage was no longer the entrée while Grae was the side dish. Everything was equal between the three of them. As it should be.

She'd always been fascinated by her brother's unconventional relationship, and here she was a few years later, in one of her very own. Damn, she couldn't be happier. And satisfied. She didn't fight the grin spreading across her face.

The relationship certainly came with some benefits.

Grae looked at her curiously, then rose out of his chair to slide behind Connor and her. Leaning in close, he whispered to the two of them, "I never told you what *my* fantasy was."

"What is it?" Connor asked, reaching back to wrap a hand around the other man's bald head affectionately.

"To be topped. And I want that person to be you, Connor, and only you."

Paige's head spun toward Grae at this revelation. She never thought he would agree to that.

Hot damn.

They might have to make their excuses and leave the barbecue early.

Paige was quite sure no one would mind...

Sign up for Jeanne's newsletter to learn about her upcoming releases, sales and more! http://www.jeannestjames.com/ newslettersignup

---

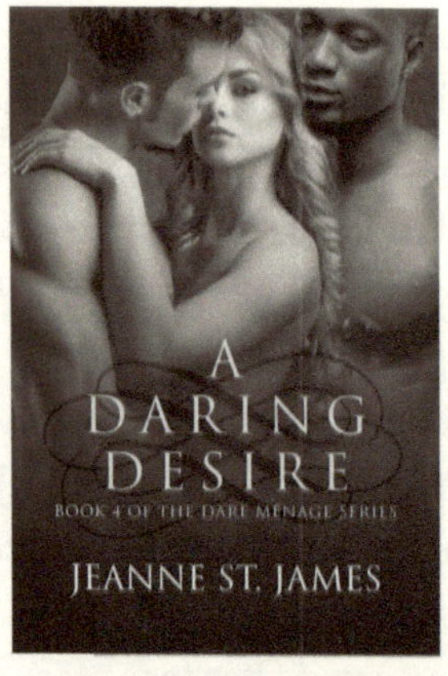

Take two defense attorneys, add one troubled NFL QB who needs them, and what do you get? Hot, sexy conflict.

Gryff Ward made a serious mistake when he hired the hot-as-hell defense attorney Rayne Jordan as an associate in his high-profile legal firm, even though she's one of the best. Now he's struggling to keep it professional, especially when she insists on calling him "Boss."

Rayne's been attracted to the firm's top attorney ever since her interview. And she's well aware that calling the conservative man "Boss" drives him crazy...in a very good way.

Add Trey Holloway, their newest client, a troubled NFL quarterback, into the mix. Tension arises when it's clear that both Gryff and Trey want Rayne, and Gryff is willing to fight for her. However, Trey doesn't hide the fact that he wants Gryff too.

Now Gryff's having a hard time fighting not only his attraction to Rayne but to another man. Even though he stubbornly refuses to admit his deepest, darkest desires.

Then Rayne takes control. She's determined to have them both in not only her bed but her life, and she won't give up until she does.

Turn the page for a sneak peek of Book 4 of The Dare Menage Series: A Daring Desire

A DARING DESIRE - CHAPTER ONE

G ryffin Ward's dick was so hard he winced.

The newest associate at his law firm stood on the other side of his desk talking. Actually *talking* to him.

He had no clue what she was even saying.

As he watched her lips move, he regretted hiring her. Even though she came highly recommended.

Rayne's stats were so good he would've been a fool not to. The more cases his practice won, the more clients they attracted. The more clients they drew, the larger his firm grew. Which meant—

Oh fuck. Who cared what it meant. Right now, he desperately needed to adjust himself because his erection was caught in his pants in a painful position.

"So, what do you think, Boss?"

Holy fuck with that "Boss" shit again.

She needed to start dressing like a nun and stop calling him that. Otherwise, he would have permanent blue balls.

What did he think? He didn't. All the blood in his brain had rushed to his dick, so he had no valid thoughts.

"You don't have to call me Boss. In fact, please don't."

"I know I don't." With a smile, Rayne leaned over and tapped him under the chin before spinning on the heel of her fuck-me pumps and heading toward the door. "But, I like it," she threw over her shoulder.

Me, too.

He took one last glance at her tight skirt with the slit in the back, the one that hugged her luscious ass and those stockings she wore with the line up the back of her legs, before she disappeared, leaving his office door open.

Gryff closed his eyes and blew out a breath.

Fuuuuuuuuuuuuuuuck.

No wonder she won most of her cases. The judge and the ADA's brains were probably mush after watching her pace the courtroom cross-examining witnesses on the stand.

No matter what, she was highly respected for being a great defense attorney.

But, he should fire her. He didn't dip his pen in the company ink and he wasn't going to start now. Even though she sorely tempted him.

He was a wretch. That's what he was.

He blew out another ragged breath and scrubbed his hands over his face.

"Gryff," came a female voice from the door.

He separated his fingers enough to peer through them at his secretary, Dani. "Yeah?"

"Are you okay?"

Fuck no, he wasn't okay. He was completely jacked. "Yeah." He sighed and lowered his hands to his lap to cover the evidence, just in case she came closer.

"Okay, well, your brother is on line one."

If that didn't make his dick soften, then nothing would. "Thanks. Close the door, please."

She gave him a little smile and did as she was told. Now, there was a woman he could work with and not lose his mind. But then

Dani dressed conservatively, like she actually worked in an office for a high profile law firm. Unlike Rayne.

With a quick adjustment to his deflating manhood, he picked up the handset and jabbed the button for line one. "What's up, big brother?"

"Hey, what's up with you?" his older brother, Grae, returned.

If his brother only knew what had just been up.

Ever since Grae hooked up with his lovers, Paige and Connor, the man had definitely lost some of his stick-up-his-ass disposition and now sounded more relaxed. His proper English had relaxed a little bit, too. But then, Paige had a filthy mouth and cursed like a sailor, so it didn't surprise him that some of that rubbed off on Grae. It was about time his brother loosened up.

"I need a favor," Grae continued.

Damn. Grae never asked for anything. His squared-away older brother couldn't possibly be having any legal problems, could he?

"Shoot."

"I've got a player—"

Ah, fuck.

"That needs representation."

Another bad boy football player getting into a jam. Nothing new. But Grae coming to him for help was.

"And you're the best."

Gryff frowned. "Are you trying to butter me up?"

"Yes. He needs your help. He's a great player and our team needs him, but he's been suspended until this little legal *snag* is cleared up."

"How little?"

"Minuscule."

"Bullshit."

"The judge wants to make an example out of him since he doesn't like professional athletes getting away with stuff like this."

Stuff like this. The words domestic and assault ping-ponged through Gryff's head. "Did he smack around his wife or girlfriend?"

"No."

"Stop beating around the bush, Grae. This isn't like you."

A pause came from the other end of the line.

"What's the charge?" Gryff prodded.

"Aggravated assault."

Gryff pursed his lips and leaned back in his leather office chair, staring up at the ceiling. "Who's the judge?"

"Thompkins."

Gryff sat up with a snap. *Shit.* He didn't want to hear the name of that hard ass and he was pretty certain he didn't want to know the answer to the next question. "Who is it?"

"Trey Holloway."

Gryff closed his eyes and cursed silently. "No."

Trey Holloway had been in the news one too many times in the past few years. The guy seemed to be spinning out of control and it didn't surprise Gryff that he'd been charged with agg assault.

"It was self-defense."

"Sure it was." Gryff ground the heel of his palm into his right eye. He had the start of a blistering headache.

"I believe him," Grae said softly. "Look, I know the guy has some issues. He's a wild child, but he's good on the field. He's got potential to take us to the Super Bowl this upcoming season. I don't want to see him throw it away."

"Are you doing this for the team? Or for him?"

Another hesitation, then, "Both. One can help the other."

Maybe. But, a troublemaker on the team had the potential to make it implode, too. If anyone knew that, Grae should. And Gryff was sure he did know it. Why was Grae putting his neck on the line for this guy? Why was this guy different than any other player who got arrested for doing something stupid?

"Talk to me," Gryff said.

"He was at a bar—"

Yeah. That's how all the good stories began.

"And he came onto a guy—"

"He's gay?" Well, Gryff never expected that.

Grae ignored his question and continued, "They were outside behind the bar making out—"

Making out. Like teenagers?

"And the guy's friends caught them. When that happened, the guy accused Trey of forcing himself on him, since the guy wasn't out. The guy acts indignant and punches Trey to make the cover story look good. The guy's friends jump in, thumping on Trey, outnumbering him. But, Trey fights back and ends up taking all four guys down, injuring a couple of them pretty badly."

"Damn," Gryff whispered, picturing the whole thing in his head as his brother explained it.

"Right. But, it's Trey's word against the other four. No one else in the bar witnessed it and if they did, they haven't come forward. Trey claims it was self-defense and I believe him. No one in their right mind takes on four guys for the hell of it."

Unless they're drunk. "Was he the only one arrested?"

"He was the only one standing in the end."

"Damn," Gryff whispered, again. "From what I've heard about him, you'd think Trey would have a lawyer on retainer."

"He does. But this is life or death right now. Like I said, there's no one better than you."

"Life or death?"

"Of his career."

Gryff spun his chair around to stare out of the window behind him. "Well, if that isn't some pressure…"

"You can handle it."

"I need some time to think about it."

"There's no time."

"Why? When is the—"

A throat cleared behind him. He looked over his shoulder and stared right into Trey Holloway's sky blue eyes. The guy gave him a wink and a cocky smile.

Get the fuck out of here.

"Grae," Gryff said in a menacing tone.

His brother chuckled. "I was going to warn you."

"Not fast enough."

"Yes, well—" and then the phone went dead.

Son of a bitch. He was going to kill his brother.

Gryff slowly turned his chair back around and carefully hung up the phone when he really wanted to smash it fifty times into the cradle until it exploded. But, he was civilized. He couldn't lose his shit in front of a client.

Even if it *was* Trey Holloway.

Gryff clearly needed to have a talk with Dani about just letting clients walk into his office without being announced or even invited in.

He studied the man standing in the middle of his office. His blue eyes looked lighter due to his dark tan. His dirty blond hair, streaked with highlights, whether fake or real, almost reached his shoulders. Scruff covered his jaw. The man was definitely built like a quarterback and not a linebacker. He wore a white button down shirt that emphasized his coloring, with the sleeves rolled up past his elbows and tucked into well-fitting jeans. Well-worn pointed cowboy boots covered feet that could move him downfield quickly when necessary.

"Like what you see?"

Gryff leveled his gaze at him. "I don't do men."

"Do they do you?"

Gryff pursed his lips and wondered if he should administer Trey's next ass whipping. Though, like the last time, it probably wouldn't do any good. He shook his head. "I don't swing that way."

"Never say never. Your brother does. Maybe it's in the genes."

Gryff's fingers clenched the arms of his office chair. So much for polite introductions. "You fuck a lot of men, Trey?"

Trey quickly hid his surprise at the unexpected question. It was there one second and then gone the next, covered by the wide smile he plastered across his face. "You mean over my lifetime or in one night?"

Trey was trying to shock him, get a rise out of him. Two could play at that game.

"How many men have you had in one night?"

Trey lifted his hands up and spread his fingers. "I don't have enough fingers to count."

"If needed, you can use your toes, too."

The corners of Trey's lips twitched. "You've got a better sense of humor than your brother."

"You don't hear me laughing."

Then they flat lined. Trey studied Gryff for a moment then gave a sharp nod. "We got off on the wrong foot." He shoved his hand out. "Trey Holloway."

Gryff didn't take the offered hand nor did he even bother to glance at it. "I know who you are. Sit down."

Trey cocked an eyebrow but parked his ass in one of the seats meant for real clients. Not an irresponsible jackass like the one in front of him.

He propped his feet on Gryff's desk. *What. The. Fuck.*

"Get your filthy boots off my desk. Put your feet on the floor, sit up straight, and act like you have some sense."

Trey's feet dropped to the floor and he scooted back in the chair with sudden color in his cheeks. He cleared his throat. "Thanks for taking my case."

Now, it was Gryff's turn to cock a brow. "I didn't say yes, yet."

"I've been falsely accused."

"That's what the guilty always say."

"Hey, I was the victim."

"Sure."

Trey crossed his arms over his chest. "Your brother says you're the best."

"I am."

Trey hooked an ankle over his knee and smiled. "What's it going to take?"

"You keeping your ass clean and a five hundred-thousand-dollar retainer."

Trey's eyes widened and he whistled softly.

Ah, see? Two could play at the shock and awe game. "If you fuck up, you lose the retainer."

"So it's insurance."

"You catch on quick."

Trey shook his head. "Just 'cause I play football doesn't mean I'm stupid."

"We'll see about that."

"Hey, Boss," Rayne burst in through the open doorway staring at a file as she walked, then stopped dead when she glanced up and spotted Trey. "Oh. Sorry. I didn't realize you were with anyone." Gryff didn't miss her green eyes widen when she recognized who sat in his office. "*Oh.*"

Yeah, *oh.*

Gryff's eyes narrowed as he watched her fingers brush over her hair, as if fixing it. There was nothing to fix, her long dark blonde hair always seems to have a 'just woke' look that fit her personality.

"You're Trey Holloway," she breathed.

Gryff frowned at the sudden color in her cheeks and the hungry look in her eyes.

Trey pushed himself to his feet and offered her his hand. Well, the guy may have some manners yet. "Yes, ma'am."

"Ma'am? Oh please." She almost giggled. *Giggled.* The corners of her lips curved as she curled her fingers around his.

Gryff's gaze glued to their hands. Hands that weren't shaking in greeting, just holding. Did his finger tickle her palm? Trey gave her a suggestive smile and raised her hand to his mouth, kissing her knuckles. "And you are?"

That seemed to jump start Rayne. "Oh, uh... Rayne. Rayne Jordan."

"Nice to meet you, Ms. Jordan."

"Uh, just Rayne." Holy shit, she just batted her eyelashes at him.

Gryff coughed loudly and both their heads spun toward him. "Trey, take a seat. Rayne, what do you need?"

"Oh, it can wait, Boss."

She didn't move to leave. Oh, hell no. Instead, she moved to stand almost directly in front of Trey's chair and parked her ass on the edge of Gryff's desk. Just like that.

"Are you a new client?" Rayne asked Trey. Was she panting?

"Yes," he said, giving her a blinding smile.

Trey was the kind of guy who thought his looks and charm would get him through life. He needed a rude awakening. You'd think after getting arrested—and not for the first time—with a felony assault, a good ass kicking and then being suspended from the team, would have done it. Apparently not.

"We don't know yet," Gryff corrected. "We're still talking terms."

Without breaking eye contact with Rayne, Trey said, "There's nothing to talk about. I'll meet the terms."

A muscle in Gryff's jaw jumped. And jumped again. He was going to kill his brother.

Get A Daring Desire (The Dare Menage, Book 4) here: www. books2read.com/ADaringDesire

IF YOU ENJOYED THIS BOOK

Thank you for reading Dare to be Three, the third book in The Dare Ménage Series. If you enjoyed it, please consider leaving a review on your favorite retailer and/or Goodreads to let other readers know. Reviews are always appreciated and just a few words can help an independent author like me tremendously!

ALSO BY JEANNE ST. JAMES

Find my complete reading order here:

https://www.jeannestjames.com/reading-order

* Available in Audiobook

<u>Standalone Books:</u>

<u>Made Maleen: A Modern Twist on a Fairy Tale</u> *

<u>Damaged</u> *

<u>Rip Cord: The Complete Trilogy</u> *

Everything About You (A Second Chance Gay Romance) *

Reigniting Chase (An M/M Standalone) *

<u>Brothers in Blue Series:</u>

<u>Brothers in Blue: Max</u> *

<u>Brothers in Blue: Marc</u> *

<u>Brothers in Blue: Matt</u> *

<u>Teddy: A Brothers in Blue Novelette</u> *

<u>Brothers in Blue: A Bryson Family Christmas</u> *

<u>The Dare Ménage Series:</u>

<u>Double Dare</u> *

<u>Daring Proposal</u> *

<u>Dare to Be Three</u> *

<u>A Daring Desire</u> *

<u>Dare to Surrender</u> *

<u>A Daring Journey</u> *

<u>**Blood & Bones: Blood Fury MC®:**</u>

<u>Blood & Bones: Trip</u> *

<u>Blood & Bones: Sig</u> *

<u>Blood & Bones: Judge</u> *

Blood & Bones: Deacon *

Blood & Bones: Cage *

Blood & Bones: Shade *

Blood & Bones: Rook *

Blood & Bones: Rev *

Blood & Bones: Ozzy

Blood & Bones: Dodge

Blood & Bones: Whip

Blood & Bones: Easy

Beyond the Badge: Blue Avengers MC™:

Beyond the Badge: Fletch

Beyond the Badge: Finn

Beyond the Badge: Decker

Beyond the Badge: Rez

Beyond the Badge: Crew

Beyond the Badge: Nox

<u>**COMING SOON!**</u>

Double D Ranch (An MMF Ménage Series)

Dirty Angels MC®: The Next Generation

WRITING AS J.J. MASTERS

The Royal Alpha Series:

(A gay mpreg shifter series)

The Selkie Prince's Fated Mate *

The Selkie Prince & His Omega Guard *

The Selkie Prince's Unexpected Omega *

The Selkie Prince's Forbidden Mate *

The Selkie Prince's Secret Baby *

ABOUT THE AUTHOR

JEANNE ST. JAMES is a USA Today bestselling romance author who loves an alpha male (or two). She was only thirteen when she started writing and her first paid published piece was an erotic story in Playgirl magazine. Her first romance novel, Banged Up, was published in 2009. She is happily owned by farting French bulldogs. She writes M/F, M/M, and M/M/F ménages.

Want to read a sample of her work? Download a sampler book here: BookHip.com/MTQQKK

To keep up with her busy release schedule check her website at www.jeannestjames.com or sign up for her newsletter: http://www.jeannestjames.com/newslettersignup

www.jeannestjames.com
jeanne@jeannestjames.com

Newsletter: http://www.jeannestjames.com/newslettersignup
Jeanne's Down & Dirty Book Crew: https://www.facebook.com/groups/JeannesReviewCrew/
TikTok: https://www.tiktok.com/@jeannestjames

facebook.com/JeanneStJamesAuthor
amazon.com/author/jeannestjames
instagram.com/JeanneStJames
bookbub.com/authors/jeanne-st-james
goodreads.com/JeanneStJames
pinterest.com/JeanneStJames

Get a FREE Sampler Book

This book contains the first chapter of a variety of my books. This will give you a taste of the type of books I write and if you enjoy the first chapter, I hope you'll be interested in reading the rest of the book.

Each book I list in the sampler will include the description of the book, the genre, and the first chapter, along with links to find out more. I hope you find a book you will enjoy curling up with!

Get it here: BookHip.com/MTQQKK

www.ingramcontent.com/pod-product-compliance
Lightning Source LLC
Chambersburg PA
CBHW031238210726

48287CB00003B/815